PUFFIN BOOKS · *Editor: Kaye Webb*

VIKING'S DA~~WN~~

No one knows q~~uite~~ ~~vi~~kings
their great thirst ~~sailin~~g the seas in their wooden
longships, whether it was to seek new fishing grounds, or
lands to colonize, or rich treasure. For young Harald
Sigurdson and the crew of the *Nameless*, the goal was
treasure, and in their fine new ship they sought it in
defiance of icy seas, incredible hardships and blood-thirsty
resistance.

Thorkell Fairhair was the leader; and black Ragnar his
half-loyal half-treacherous blood brother, whose insatiable
greed threatened to bring disaster on them all. Many times
on this harsh and lonely voyage Harald witnessed
incredible courage and brutality; comrades were swept
away by the towering seas, others died bravely in battle
during forays on land, and with his skin scoured from his
body by the wind, or clinging to a sinking vessel, he
wondered if he would ever see again his father and the
fjords of his homeland.

Into this breathlessly gripping story is woven the true
spirit of the vikings – their ruthlessness and their loyalty,
their immense hardiness. Even their cruelty becomes
understandable in times which were themselves so cruel,
and their bravery can rarely have been equalled. For any
reader of nine and over this book, the first of Henry
Treece's famous trilogy, offers a chance, in the course of a
masterly story, to understand a dramatic epoch of history.
Harald Sigurdson's later adventures can be read in *The
Road to Miklagard*.

Cover design by Victor Ambrus

Viking's Dawn

Henry Treece

Illustrated by Christine Price

Puffin Books in association
with The Bodley Head

Puffin Books: a Division of
Penguin Books Ltd, Harmondsworth,
Middlesex, England
Penguin Books Australia Ltd, Ringwood,
Victoria, Australia
Penguin Books Canada Ltd,
41 Steelcase Road West,
Markham, Ontario, Canada
Penguin Books (N.Z.) Ltd
182–190 Wairau Road,
Auckland 10, New Zealand

First published by The Bodley Head 1955
Published in Puffin Books 1967
Reprinted 1971, 1972, 1974
Copyright © the Estate of Henry Treece, 1955

Made and printed in Great Britain by
C. Nicholls & Company Ltd
Set in Linotype Juliana

Contents

About this Book

This is the story of a voyage made by a shipload of north-men about the year A.D. 780, before the regular viking invasions on Britain began. In this book the word 'viking' means 'a sea-traveller,' though it can also be taken to imply 'a dweller along the wicks,' or fjords. 'To go a-viking, therefore is to go on a voyage.

Who were the northmen? It is perhaps wrong of us to think of them as being definitely Norsemen or Danes or Swedes or Finns or Lapps. At this stage in their history they had not fully developed those differences in nation-ality which they have today. Though, of course, there was some dissimilarity, especially in their folk-tales and myths. Horic's wind-tying, and his trick with the beetle, both belong to Lapp folklore; while Thorkell's tale about the vikings who discussed the after-life while waiting to be beheaded comes from a Norse Saga.

What manner of men were these northmen? They are often described as being bloodthirsty pirates and nothing else. Yet it is worth noting that when they had settled in this country they became some of its most law-abiding inhabitants. Moreover, their wonderful sagas show that their literature was a highly cultivated one; the splendid construction of their longships demonstrates their intelligence and ingenuity. No doubt they *were* fierce and reckless; yet it must be remembered that they had to face equally fierce and reckless enemies. Had the vikings not possessed such qualities, they would not have left their enduring name on the pages of history as they have done.

But why did the northmen suddenly decide to go a-viking, after centuries of quiet living? Historians have a number of answers to this question. Some say that the Scandinavian countries were becoming overpopulated and that the vikings sought new homes. Yet it is a strange thing that, in the early stages at least, after making their raids, they then returned to their own homes. Other scholars say that the vikings were some of the most independent northmen, who wished to get away from the new centralized governments that were being set up at home. Still others put forward the theory that the northmen were carrying on a great battle against Christianity, which was at last threatening to engulf them. Such experts see the viking invasions as being 'the last great effort of Odin to limit the dominion of Christ.' Yet, once again, it is worth noting that when they became Christians, the vikings were only too anxious to spread their new faith, even to the extent of chopping off the heads of those who would not forsake Odin !

It is all a great enigma. Perhaps those historians who say that the vikings sailed simply because the herring on which they fed had moved to other places are as near as anyone else in solving the problem. But what we do know without any doubt is that they *did* sail and, in sailing, created a great sea tradition which we British have inherited from them; for the blood of Aun and Harald and Thorkell runs in our veins too.

This book sets out to tell the story of one of the earliest voyages, not one of the great journeys, for it happens before the sea-rovers had a very clear idea of the broader world about them. Yet it was a pioneer voyage, and so full of unforeseen dangers. It is the tale of one longship, on one voyage.

In our world, when we are used to big aircraft making their daily trips across the Atlantic, month in and month out, we perhaps forget those early pioneers who flew ten miles – and then no more. We admire those prairie schooners that passed over the wide spaces, from one side of America to the other; but do we ever give a thought to those wagons – small worlds of wood and canvas to their occupants, like our longship – whose wheels and shafts lay, bleached like bones among the cactus in the cruel sunlight, after the Indians had fired them?

Nowadays, perhaps too many of us long for immediate glory. We ignore, and even despise, those who do not quite 'make the grade'. Yet they are often the pioneers, because of whose hard efforts later adventurers find an easier success. Someone must set the ball rolling, whoever scores with it afterwards!

Have you ever seen the painting which shows an incident in the boyhood of Raleigh? In it an old sea-dog is telling the boy about the adventures to be met with on the high seas. Young Raleigh sits, cross-legged and wide-eyed. The old sailorman passes on his experience to one who will make a more glorious use of it one day. But who was that old man?

Perhaps, when you have read this, you may see the importance of Thorkell and the many others who went to Valhalla. And perhaps you will understand Harald better. I hope so.

HENRY TREECE

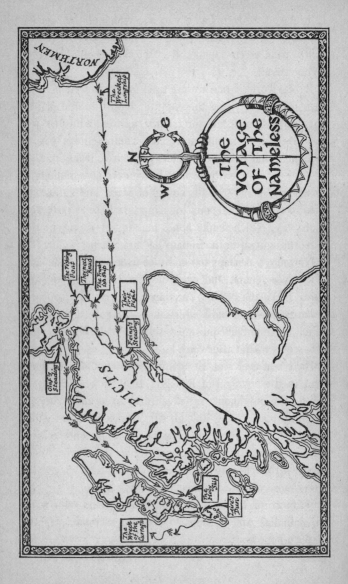

Chapter I *The Hall by the Tarn*

Two figures stood in the darkness, a man and a boy. Behind them the pine woods sighed, as though overcome by a great and unnameable sadness, the melancholy sound made by all ancient forests. As the round moon came from behind a bank of cloud, throwing its silver light over the rough and rocky land below, the two figures peered down into the valley beneath them, their heavy cloaks sweeping away from them in the night-wind that blew towards them from the woods. A great white sea-bird circled above their heads, crying harshly and pitifully in the moonlight. They shuddered at the sound, looking up in dread. The man's bearded lips moved silently, as though he spoke a charm against the witches of the night. The moon slowly withdrew behind the straggling cloudbank, and for a moment there was utter darkness once more.

Then suddenly, from the valley, came a surge of flame, a great red and orange spurting-up of light. A thick cloud of oily smoke rose above it, into the night air. A flock of birds flew, twittering up from the valley, to the woods. The two watchers drew in their breath as the many wings beat above them in the darkness.

Now the fire-glow spread and its angry light flared out over a black tarn nearby, so that the man and boy saw reflected in the sombre water every shape and hue of the flames.

The man licked his lips and said, 'His hall burns well, son. When we laid the logs for him, I did not think we should see such a sending-off fire.'

The boy said, 'Such a king as he does not deserve a funeral fire like that. A king who has no ship to take him to Odin is not worth following. Better a man should go a-viking for himself.'

The man looked angry for a space. Then he smiled and said, 'It would go hard with us old ones if you young cocks ruled the world! Gudröd could not help being a poor man. There are too many kings in the land, lad; and not all of them can be rich men. My choice fell out badly, to pledge myself to a poor man, that is all. Yet, no doubt, Odin will receive Gudröd in Valhalla no less courteously because he sails there in a burning house than if he came in a longship!'

The boy frowned and said, 'You served him too faithfully, Father. We should have left him before the famine came. When his corn failed, we should have gone to the coastwise Norse and lived off fish. The herring never fail.'

Now the fire had reached its height and began to slacken. The air about the two was filled with the smell of acrid smoke. Small burnt particles and ashes fell about them. The man wiped his hand across his forehead. His gold arm-ring flashed in the glow. He said, 'Who is to know? One day the herring might go away. Then what will the fishers do? They will have neither corn nor fish, Harald. How shall a Norseman live then, think you?'

'He will live on his wits, as Odin meant him to, Father,' said the boy. 'There are other lands and other folk who have plenty. The Danes have plenty, so have the English. Or a man could voyage overland and take his bread from the Romans. There is no need to starve, Father.'

Now the blaze below them was sinking to a dull glow and the birds were flying back from the wood towards the tarn's dark waters.

The man said, 'Life is never sure, Harald. Whichever way a man turns, he thinks he might have done better to take the other path.'

The boy frowned and shut his eyes tight, as though squeezing the sudden tears from them. 'If we had left Gudröd sooner, my mother and brothers might still be alive with us. They would not have died in the famine.'

The man made an impatient movement under his cloak, almost as though his hand would strike the boy, but he answered calmly, 'Only Odin knows whether that is true, son. We might have lost them in a village-burning if we had gone to the coast. They might have been chosen as sacrifices when the fishing went badly. We do not know. At least, old Gudröd did not call for sacrifices. That much can be said for him.'

The boy's voice was bitter. 'No, he knew which side his bread was buttered. He had so few followers left that he could not afford to lay any of them on the stones. He might have had to do a hand's turn himself, if he had done.'

The man turned away from him, impatiently. 'Come, Harald,' he said. 'We will make the best of a bad job and find another lord to follow.'

They made their way towards the dark woods, and only once did they turn back to glance at the dying embers of Gudröd's great hall. As the pine-trees enfolded them the man said, 'This way lies the fjord, if the beasts of the forest will let us pass.'

The boy said, 'Better to become the bear's supper than to remain the cow's slave.'

The man smiled grimly, 'Who shall say that but one who has found himself on the bear's dish?'

They spoke no more as they pushed past the overhanging boughs and went into the deep darkness of the forest.

Chapter 2 *Thorkell Fairhair*

The fjord was full of the noise of busy men. The very air seemed to vibrate as in a great open-air smithy. The clanging of anvil-blows, the hammering of planks, the buzzing of long two-handed saws echoed and re-echoed across the enclosed blue water. And all these sounds seemed to glance like flat stones over the surface of the sea-valley, to lose themselves up the farther rocky slopes and then in the great dim forests that crowned the rim of the inlet and stretched far away into the mountains, into the unknown frightening spaces of trolls and witches.

The little thatch and wooden settlement that straggled along the shore of the fjord throbbed with activity. Black-faced men in leather aprons worked the great ox-skin bellows to fan the flames of many outdoor furnaces; others beat out long iron nails on anvils that were gripped between their padded knees; yet others walked backwards down long rope-walks, twisting the harsh fibres in their raw hands. The women worked busily stitching, with thick waxed thread, or at the shuttles of their looms, which were set up outside the hovel doors so as to make the most of the new and welcome spring light. Children scurried back and forth, fetching and carrying for their sweating elders, sometimes a hammer, or a pail of ice-cold water to temper the iron, sometimes a roughly-cut hunk of barley bread or a pannikin of corn-wine.

All worked in that place, even the very old and the

crippled. The ship they were building was not the toy of one man; it was the property of them all. And it was almost finished. Another day at the most would see it ready for the painters. Even the oldest ones, plaiting thongs, horny-handed in the shadow, saw new dreams of gold taking shape before their dim eyes. 'Share and share alike,' thought they. 'To each his portion, and may she speed well and return laden before I make my greetings to Odin.' This longship had been built by the whole village. Those who were skilled in shipbuilding had worked day by day, with an adze on the planks or walking backwards along the rope-walks. Those who had no such skill, or were too old to wield an axe or to ply a needle, had contributed in other ways, either by supplying food and drink to their more active neighbours, or by paying good money to shipwrights to come from afar.... And all this, so that the ship should bring back profit to the village. These men did not think of glory, or even of adventure. They were practical men – as most northerners are – who wanted a good return for their labour or money. And the ship which they were creating would bring back those good returns, they hoped. This village had heard of the rich court of the Franks. They had seen the fine silks and the painted pictures that had come from Byzantium. And such English noblemen as had crossed the northern seas to them had worn gold about their necks and arms.... The rest of the world must be very rich, they thought.

And so they built this longship, to relieve the rest of the world of some of its surplus riches. The village on the fjord could do with a little gold, and some silks. It would not even object to a few pictures – provided, of course, that the artist had used real gold leaf in painting them!

Among all these fjord-folk, the longship lay on her runway like a royal thing, a proud princess whose slaves attended to her every want. A longship that would brave the harsh buffeting of the open seas, or out-trick the subtlest of rivers. A handsome shell in which a warrior king would feel proud to drift out on an ebb tide, the death-flames licking round him as he lay among his furs and his weapons and his hounds, on that last long journey to Odin's feast-hall.

Of clean and fresh-smelling oak, the longship was almost eighty feet long, from stem to stern, and sixteen feet broad at her middle. Standing over seven feet high from keel-bottom to gunwales, she dwarfed the many busy men who toiled about her on the stocks, even though as yet her forty-foot mast had not been stepped into its socket in the keel. They smiled at each other, satisfied with their work. If the good weather held, they would step the mast tomorrow, so that it would fall backwards quickly and easily when the forestay was eased off. And tomorrow, by the help of all the gods in the groves, they would fit the other ropes, the stays to prow and stern, those that braced the long yard-arm, those that ran on pulleys to raise and lower the sail. . . .

The foreman of the shipwrights wiped a rough and work-soiled hand over his red face. He turned to the apprentice lad who caulked the smart clinker-built planking of the sides.

'Never was maiden more comely,' he said. 'Trust a horse before a hound, a hound before a lass – and a longship before them all!' The boy grinned back at him. 'Maybe you are right, Master Björn,' he said. 'But women can be useful at times! My aunt and my sisters have woven the sail for her, and a fine thing it is – all red and blue and green, in great stripes the thickness of a pine-trunk.'

'Ay, and your mother has embroidered the pennant, hasn't she, lad?' said Björn, smiling.

The boy looked down, as though he knew not what to say. 'Well, Master,' he ventured at last, 'she has edged it and put on its long golden fringe, but no one has told her what emblem to work on the white silk. It rests as unmarked as the snows on the Bear Mountain. We know not what name she shall carry.'

He glanced at Björn craftily, as though expecting his master to give him the answer. But Björn only whistled and bent to examine a row of rivets and their great square washers that held the long oak planks fast together.

'Ay, ay,' he said, in a whisper, 'who knows what she will be named!'

The boy was suddenly conscious of a hush about him. He stopped working and bent towards Björn. 'Here is the one, Master, who will know, if anyone does.'

Björn turned and then pulled his forelock, and, like all the other workmen, stood silent and waiting. And among the huts by the blue water a name was whispered that fetched the young maids to the doorways, and put a smile on the faces of the older women.

'Thorkell Fairhair! Thorkell Fairhair!'

In the shadow of one hut an old man sat, patiently mending a fish-net. His hands were gnarled and twisted with rheumatism, but he forced them on and on, to tie the knots in the tarry twine. A long sword-cut had once ploughed the length of his cheek and had taken away the teeth on one side of his jaw. He heard the name, this old warrior, and a shiver seemed to pass over his face like a little cloud before the sun. His battle-scarred face wrinkled along its war-cuts in a strange, ironic smile.

'Ay, Thorkell Fairhair, the maids call him, knowing but his beauty ! Thorkell Skullsplitter is his name in other parts.'

He shrugged and went on mending the net, his head shaking a little with a palsy brought on by the bitter wind that blew along the fjord for the greater part of the year.

The young man, Thorkell, stood among the silent folk. He was but of medium height, and slimly made. As yet he wore no moustaches or beard, and his blue eyes looked out of his smooth face as mildly as a girl's. Only there was something in the thin twist of his lips that took away from the gentleness. Something in the lean twitching of his jaws that spoke of tireless nervous energy. Something in the quick catlike tread that told its own tale of sudden action. Those who noted only the long corn-golden hair that hung, unplaited down his back, down the gilded mail shirt, would have been deceived, thought Björn.

Those who noted only the many glittering rings that circled his long slim fingers, the thick arm-bands that clasped his arms, the gold gorget at his throat, would have been deceived, thought the apprentice lad, with a secret grin. This was no maid; this was Thorkell, call him by whatever name you cared or dared, but Thorkell.

And when Thorkell came to the village, men were silent until he gave the word to speak. Even the old warriors, men who had killed bears in the high summer on the mountain tops. Some said he was the son of an outlawed king; some said he was a king himself, of another land beyond Ultima Thule; some, the oldest ones who had lost their grip on the life of ordinary men, whispered that Odin had sent him down among the Northmen to see what they were up to and to report back when he had seen. But when one too-daring young warrior in his cups had called him 'Thorkell Odinson' to his face, he had kicked the fool's feet from under him and had come near to throttling him with those same slim, ring-laden fingers. . . . So no one really knew what to think. And now Thorkell Whoever-he-was stood looking at the longship, looking and smiling faintly, out of those cold blue eyes, that seemed to see beyond the hull, beyond the ice-blue fjord, beyond the farther hills and forests, and on and on, beyond the very rim of the world herself. . . .

Behind him stood another one. His sacking cloak hung as limply as the rough red hair that he had plaited loosely and had braided with leather shoe-laces; a tall thin man, with the nose of a hawk and the quick eyes of a ferret. A man who was constantly scratching his side or poking a bony finger into his great red ears. This was a different sort of man. He wore no mail shirt, but a long leather jerkin, plated here and there with strips of iron to act as armour of a sort. About his thin waist he wore a rusting chain – not a gilt-studded belt, like Thorkell's. But from that chain hung something more terrifying than the red-sheathed longsword that Thorkell bore; a mace of bog-oak, into which a score of sharp flints had been sunk, each one jutting horribly forth, its sharpest point outward. This was a weapon to fear in all truth. The sword is deadly, but its work is done in a minute. Such a thing as this man wore might bring the torments of the damned upon a man before Odin smiled down on him and gave him some relief.

The villagers saw the mace, saw the strange, sad, sheep-like face of the man as he scratched his thin hair or shuffled his high shoulders as though the nibbling-ants were at him. 'Wolf Water-hater,' they said. 'Wolf who has never washed in his life and vows to stay like that until his time comes!'

And even the children giggled and pushed closer to see this Wolf, who had sailed on every sea man knew, yet hated the very thought of water touching his tender skin!

Then the long silence was broken. Thorkell turned his head towards the tall man. 'Is she fair?' he asked, laconically.

Wolf stepped forward so pompously that even the apprentice lad smiled. He went onwards, his pale eyebrows raising and lowering themselves, and seemed to look at the longship as though he had never seen one before.

He stopped and poked his red finger into one of the sixteen oar-ports that ran along each side of the ship in the third strake from the top. They were not round holes, but long narrow ones. Wolf ran his finger along them for a while, then turned and said, 'Cut off the shipmaster's thumbs; he is too lazy to carve a circle.'

There was a stir among the folk. Björn was a true Norseman and did not wait for anyone to ask where he was. He stepped down from his plank and nodded to Thorkell. Then he waited for the other to speak. Thorkell said, 'Shall we cut them off with your own knife or with mine?' He drew a long thin blade from his girdle. The haft was set with coral, noted Björn. The village folk drew in their breath. The children were secretly

cuffed into silence. The old man mending the net shrugged his shoulders and licked his forefinger to twist another knot, as though he had heard it all before and thought it little worth the noting.

Björn said, 'Yours, Thorkell. Mine is too tarry from the ropes.' He held out his hand for Thorkell's knife. It was a pretty one and Björn was curious to see how it was made. Thorkell handed it to him and the shipmaster examined it carefully and then returned it with a smile. 'Not much good against a wolf, I should say,' he said.

Thorkell said, 'You are wrong, Björn. If you were to keep your thumbs, I would bet you a horse against a yard of rope that this knife is just the thing to probe beneath a spring bear's fat.'

He went towards Björn to illustrate what he was saying. 'Look, the blade is thin and keen. You just slip it under his arm as he grasps, and you roll sideways, like this, and then he falls, but you must be ready to jump back for he weighs heavier than a chariot! He would crunch your leg like a winter stick!'

As he said this he made the movements of the hunter, while Björn pretended to be the bear waked from his hibernation. The folk stood stock-still, sucking in their breath with expectation, for they were simple northern folk who readily gave themselves to a tale.

Thorkell thrust with his thin knife, and the strong-armed Björn watched and twisted sideways as the hunter twisted. And the bear held the knife clasped firm beneath his arm-pit. Thorkell was trapped!

So long the two held this lock that a child said, 'Mother, the men are silly with the new sun. I want my milk, mother! Milk, mother!'

Then Thorkell let his knife fall on the pebbled shore of the fjord. He straightened up and smiled. Björn straightened up and smiled too. Then Björn stooped and picked up Thorkell's knife and gave it back to him.

'Here are my thumbs,' he said.

Thorkell said, 'Wolf, you are a fool. You should go back to the Caledonians and say that you are a fool. Björn is a sensible man. He has bear's blood in him, like all proper Northmen. Björn will tell you why the oar-holes are not round.'

Björn said, 'Master Thorkell, saving your presence, Wolf is a fairly sensible man for a Pict, but he is hasty. That is all. The oar-holes are not round because my lad here has sense. In truth, he has never sailed farther across the water than this fjord, but he has sense. This is his idea, "When you have the sail up," says he, "you do not need the oars, Master." I spoke him fair and agreed with him. "All right," says he. "When you pull in the oar, what have you left?" "A hole," says I. "Right," says he, "then make your hole flat and straight, so that an oar can come into the ship by it, allowing for the blade. Then make a little shutter over the flat hole, and you have got rid of the fear of water!" All this said the boy, and like a fool I followed him, for the idea seemed a good one to me. And I put little shutters, as he had said, over the oar-holes, so that the ship would be safe from the waves.'

Björn moved across to the longship and pointed to the securely-bolted pieces of wood.

Thorkell watched him. Then he turned his pale blue eyes upon Wolf, slowly, steadily, with a sidelong motion of the head. And the smile on his lips was not pleasant to see. The old man in the shadows lowered his war-torn face and said, 'Aiee, Aiee, Wolf should not speak so fast!'

Thorkell said, 'Wolf, come you here, you dolt of dolts.'

Wolf shambled back from the longship as readily as he had gone to it, a smile on his thin red face, his thin red hand still scratching under his leather jerkin.

'Kneel before the shipmaster and beg his pardon,' said Thorkell, looking down at him.

The villagers stared as the thin man knelt.

'Not with his knife,' said Wolf, pleasantly. 'I would prefer yours, Thorkell. Every man can make a mistake, but that is no reason why he should suffer more than a twelve-month.'

Björn said, 'Must he take my punishment, Thorkell?'

Thorkell said, 'Who talks of punishment among a free folk such as this? A man may have a joke, may he not, without spoiling the hand of a good tradesman?'

Wolf looked down at his red scarred hands. 'What trade can these follow, Thorkell?' he said, smiling quietly.

Thorkell kicked him gently in the side and rolled him over on to the pebbles. Then Wolf rose, rubbing his long finger below his nose, with a comical expression on his face, and Thorkell put his arm about his shoulders.

'Come, side-man,' he said, 'let us drink a horn of mead in this place and think about a name for the ship.' Then as an afterthought, he said, 'Come you, shipmaster, and let us drink together, for you seem a sharp fellow.'

Björn said, 'Not I, Thorkell, but my apprentice.'

'Bring him, too,' said Thorkell. 'A lad who has thoughts about oar-holes like that should make a viking one day.'

Now she lay ready, the proud longship of the fjord. In the three days since Thorkell Fairhair had returned to the village, the master painters had been at work on her, using their bright hues to transform the smooth-planed oak to a picture of magnificent colour. Each strake of her sides was painted a different colour, red and blue and ochre. Her gunwales were gilded. Each shutter over the oar-ports was painted a deep black. Her tall mast stood silver in the sunlight. The high-flung bows and stern shone richly under a thick layer of gold-leaf, varnished with an Eastern resin to withstand the salty ravages of any deep and distant ocean. Even the platforms, fore and aft, were coloured leaf-green, with an especially durable pigment whose secret was known only to these travelling craftsmen, who journeyed here and there along the fjords at this time, selling their skill to any community that had such a venture in hand.

Thorkell Fairhair and his henchman Wolf sat at a rough table on the edge of the village, at the spot where the shore first started to run down to the fjord. On the board before them lay a heap of white knuckle-bones, perhaps four score in all. Thorkell's long sword lay beside them in its sheath, its hilt turned away from his hand so that he might only draw it at a disadvantage.

Behind the table stood the villagers, in many rows, old men, women and the children. Dogs and grunting pigs wandered here and there, some of them even stopping to rub against the trestles, or to push beneath the stools of the seated men.

Before the table stood a long line of men, some of them villagers, even men who had wielded the heavy adze on the oaken planks or dragged the giant spoke-shave along the tall mast; others were men from farther away, who had heard the news of the venture and were anxious to share the excitements of the voyage. Yet others came from beyond the fjord, from far away where different kings ruled and different gods haunted a man's dreams. Yet all were welcome to Thorkell Fairhair, whatever strange tongue they spoke, whatever the colour of their skin.

For Thorkell must gather about him forty sailors before his new longship might set her face towards the farthermost seas. Forty men who feared nothing and who used a weapon as readily as they pulled at an oar. It was not always easy to find so many men of such qualities from one small community. And now men stood before him, saying their names, and the name of their weapon, laying their hands palm upwards on the table-top so that Thorkell could judge whether they were callused enough to pull at an oar for days on end. . . . Those he rejected with a grim smile and a nod of his golden head smiled back as grimly and walked away, taking the path they had come, to find another village where a good ship was being pushed out into the fjord – for at this time a great restlessness was sweeping across the countries and men everywhere woke up with the itch to be moving. . . . Those he chose were given a pair of the knuckle-bones to keep, as sign that they were under contract to Thorkell.

They must keep these bones safely, until such time as they wished to break with him and leave the ship. Then, all they had to do was to hand them both back, putting one in his right hand and one in his left, with the words: 'The snow leaves the hills, the leaf leaves the trees, the bird leaves the nest – and I leave you.' Once the bones were given and the words spoken, neither man was under any obligation to the other, and might even kill each other should they feel the need to do so. But while the man had the bones and the words had not been said, he was bound to serve and to obey; nor might either harm the other even in the slightest degree, without becoming liable under the law of the folk-meeting to severe penalties. And these laws were strictly adhered to, even among men who might be called thieves and murderers by the rest of the world – the Christian world of the Franks and the English. . . .

'I am Rolf Wryneck, steersman, and my dagger is named Battlefang,' said a thin man who carried his head on one side and seemed to sniff with a perpetual cold.

Thorkell turned back to Wolf and both laughed. 'This man should serve us well,' said Thorkell, 'for he will be able to see round the corners before we get there! Here are the bones, Rolf Wryneck, and may you steer us well!'

'I am Gnorre Nithing, from Finland, and my sword is Grunter,' said the next man, so stooping and round-shouldered that he almost looked deformed.

Wolf said, 'Nithing is a strange name, man. It is only given to one who has broken the law and whose life is any man's to take.'

Thorkell looked at him searchingly. 'What did you do, Nithing?' he asked sternly. 'No outlaw can sail with me.'

The Finn looked piteously at Thorkell. 'Master,' he stammered, 'I killed a man. Only that.'

'Only that!' echoed Thorkell, gazing at the Finn's bent back and stooping posture. 'What was he, a straw man in the spring festival?'

The villagers began to laugh and the Finn's face went red. He stammered and could not answer. His coarse hands trembled as he laid them on the table.

'Come man, speak up,' said Wolf, half jeering.

Then the man behind the Finn pushed forward. In height and breadth he was the biggest man the village had ever seen. His harsh black hair hung down unkempt beneath his iron, horned helmet. About his massive chest he wore an untanned bearskin, pulled in to his thick waist with a length of raw-hide. A double-bladed axe swung down to the ground from the strap.

'The Nithing asks for work,' he said to Thorkell, without any sign of respect. 'He does not ask to be tried by the folk-meeting here. He killed a man who had killed his brother. But that man was a king in Finland, and so Gnorre became a Nithing. I would have killed him. Would not you?' He fixed his red-rimmed eyes on Wolf and his great black beard jutted out towards Thorkell's henchman.

There were many about the table at that moment who edged away a little and took a firmer grip on their weapons, for it was at such moments as these that a deadly fight might begin.

Wolf scratched the side of his nose calmly and came round the table. He stood within an axe-stroke of the great man and said pleasantly, 'It is peaceful up there in the woods, among the trees. Here a man can hardly

move for folk. And always there are women under his feet screaming that he will wake the baby.'

The big man smiled back grimly and said, 'I am of the woods. I get my clothes from the woods as you see. I am at home there. I know nothing of women and babies, but I will go with you to the woods.'

Now all about the table sucked in their breath for they knew what these calm words meant. Only Thorkell seemed unmoved. He said, 'Who are you to come here boasting of your prowess over bears? We have each killed a bear and do not go about parading his skin like a young man who is anxious for the girls to think him brave.'

The big man stopped smiling and said, 'I wish to call you Master, or I should answer you another way. I am Aun Doorback and this is Peacegiver.' He rattled the great axe on the table-top. 'I speak now for Gnorre Nith-

ing because he is not a man to speak for himself. He is a warrior and a viking, not a talker about firesides.'

Thorkell smiled up at him gently, 'What right have you to speak for another man, Aun Doorback?' he said.

'The best right of all, Master Goldhair,' said Aun. 'It was my brother that Gnorre killed.'

There was a murmur among the villagers.

'Did you not wish to kill Gnorre, then?' asked Thorkell.

'No, Master,' said Aun. 'If Gnorre had not killed him, I should have done, for my brother was an evil man.'

'Should you not be king in his place, then?' asked Thorkell.

Aun said, 'Yes, but when the folk-meeting judged Gnorre to be an outlaw, I could not stay and rule such a stupid people. I chose to go with Gnorre and keep men from striking him down unjustly.'

Thorkell said, 'Take you two pairs of bones, Aun. One for yourself and one for Gnorre. You may be a good man.'

But Aun would not go from the table. He turned now to Wolf. 'Have we a debt to settle?' he said.

Wolf said, 'Let me feel the weight of your axe.'

He took the great weapon and made the motion of raising it. The veins in his arms stood out and his face was red. He smiled ruefully and said, 'I pity the bear on whose skull that falls.'

He handed back the great axe.

'I will fight you with knives or not at all,' he said.

Aun burst into a great laugh and said, 'I have never used a knife but to cut my meat. I should not be able to do more than scratch at you.'

Wolf said, 'That would suit me, friend! As for me, I should burst a blood-vessel if I swung an axe big enough to match that tree-trunk.'

They looked long at each other. Then Aun held out his hand and said, 'You are too brave a man to feed the ravens. I will not send you to your death, Redhead.'

Wolf took his hand and said, 'It would be a pity to spoil such a great mound of a man with my wicked little knife.'

Thus they were friends and Wolf went back behind the table, while Aun and Gnorre drew to one side to let the next man come forward.

And so the names were given, of man and weapon: Hasting and his axe Dream-maker; Gryffi and his sword Yell-stick; Kragge and his knife Homegetter; Ivar and his axe Pretty One, and so on, along the line of men, until at last there was only one man left. Yet Thorkell still had six knuckle-bones upon the table, enough for three men.

The last man sat silently, away from the others. He seemed to be crouching upon the pebbles, as though he were busy with something that held his attention. He had forgotten where he was. All eyes turned towards him and many men laughed to see him. He was very small and his face was the yellow colour of parchment. His black hair was shaven from the sides of his head and his one long plait was wound round and round on top of his skull and held up with bone pins. His eyes were narrow and his cheekbones high.

Thorkell called to him a time or two and at last he heard and came towards the table. Then they laughed. He wore a long heavy cloak of sheepskin and trousers of reindeer hide, but they hung too low between the legs so that his appearance was that of an ape rather than a man. He walked with his toes turned in and his long arms hanging at his sides.

When he got to the table he smiled, ignoring the laughter, and stood silent. Thorkell said, 'Are you a man?'

He did not understand the question and said thickly, 'No, I think not.' All the village roared, even the children, who crowded round to see what that funny man was like.

'Look at the beads sewn on to his skin tunic,' said one child.

'Yes, but look at the great bone rings on his wrists and arms. No bear has bones big enough to make such rings. He must be a Lapp wizard,' said another.

Thorkell heard the child. 'Are you from Lapland?' he asked.

The little man smiled even more broadly and shook his head so violently that it seemed his hair would come undone and fall about his face.

Thorkell said slowly and loudly, as one who speaks to a stupid child, 'What sword do you carry?'

The Laplander made the motion of carrying a heavy load. When the men had quietened again, Thorkell said, 'Have you a weapon?' He pointed to his own sword on the table. The Laplander went forward to take it up, thinking Thorkell had given it to him. Thorkell snatched it away only just in time.

'Speak to him, Wolf,' he said. 'I do not know how to make him understand.'

Wolf came forward and took the little man by the arm and went through the dumb show of fighting with a knife, then an axe, then a sword, even of wrestling.

It was at the last that he made the mistake of gripping the Laplander's arm too tightly. It seemed that the man thought he was actually being attacked. What happened then was too fast for most of the men to see properly. First they saw Wolf smiling, and grappling in play with the Lapp. Then they saw Wolf's legs disappearing over the little man's shoulder, and Wolf stretched out on the pebbles, the breath knocked quite out of him.

The little Lapp went forward and helped him up again. Wolf rubbed his shoulder painfully and said, 'Do your own talking now, Thorkell. I had almost as soon fight Aun Doorback.'

Then Gnorre came forward and whispered in the Lapp's ear. The man grinned and went to the table, 'Horic Laplander,' he said, 'no axe, no sword, no knife. This.'

He pulled from his pouch a thin length of tarred twine. There were four knots tied in it along its length. Thorkell put out his hand, in wonder, to touch it, but the man jumped back and shook his head. Gnorre said, 'You must not touch it, Master. It is a magic thing.'

'What does he call it?' asked Wolf, bewildered.

Gnorre spoke to him again, and the man said, 'Windmaker. Horic bring whatever wind ship wants. Untie knot, wind blow; tie knot, wind go.' Then he laughed aloud and stared from one face to another, in wonder, for no one believed him.

Thorkell said, 'No good. We have too many lunatics in the ship's company already. He must go back to Lapland with his winds.'

Aun stepped forward and said, 'If you send this man away, I shall go too. He will take the good winds with him.'

And three or four other men spoke up then and said that they would follow Aun and give back the knucklebones.

Thorkell was about to tell them to go when Wolf whispered and a smile came over Thorkell's face.

'Aun,' he said, 'you seem to spend your life fighting other men's battles, but I think none the less of you for that – unless you become too great a nuisance. You must remember that I am the shipmaster. Now, I will tell you what we will do – if this Horic is as good a wizard as everybody seems to think, let him do something we can all see, something useful to our enterprise, and then I will let him sail with us, for he seems to have strength enough to row the boat himself, without any help from us !'

Gnorre spoke to Horic, telling him to make a magic that would help the ship. Horic nodded and then bent down low over the ground, seeming to search among the coarse grass for something he had lost. Everyone watched him carefully now. Even the children were still.

Horic picked up something from the ground. It was a small black beetle. He stooped then and found a twig. All men watched him as he pulled out one of the black hairs of his head and carefully tied one end round the beetle's body and the other end to the twig. Then he pushed the twig a little way into the sandy ground and sat down near to it, watching.

The beetle began to walk round the twig, trying to get away, but he was tethered by the long black hair. All he could do was to go round and round. As he walked about the twig, the hair wrapped itself shorter and shorter until the beetle was only an inch from the twig.

By now men were beginning to think that this was only a jest that the Lapp was playing on Thorkell, and they began to laugh. But the little man looked up sternly and waved them to silence. Then, as the beetle approached the twig on the end of the hair, he looked up towards the wooded hilltop, his yellow face anxious, his narrow eyes keen and watchful.

'What in Odin's name is he doing?' asked Wolf.

'He is bringing you shipmen,' said Gnorre, in a hoarse whisper.

Now Thorkell watched with great concern for he was anxious to make up a full crew before he sailed. Yet every day's delay was a serious one, for these wandering men were impatient and would hand back the bones if they did not sail quickly.

Now the Lapp was trembling with an inner excitement and Thorkell saw that the beetle had almost touched the twig.

Suddenly it moved its hard-shelled back against the slip of wood, and Horic, gazing up the hill gave a little cry of pleasure and pointed towards the woods with his yellow hand.

They all turned and followed his gaze.

From between the hanging pine-boughs two men came, a young one and an older man, staggering as though they had come far across the mountains and through the woods.

The older man's head was covered by his long cloak, but all men saw that the young one had hair the colour of corn. The two waved joyously, as though with relief, and began to descend the hill towards the village. Thorkell shook his head in wonder then held out the bones to the Lapp. For a moment his eyes were fixed beyond the world's edge and he did not see them. Then he awoke and took the bones and stood by Gnorre to watch the two come down.

Aun said, 'The young one will make a proper viking in time.'

So Harald and his father Sigurd came to the village at last.

Chapter 4 *The Ship-Naming*

In the feast hall men were merry. Spruce boughs lined the walls, turning the long log shed into a forest glade. Resinous pine-boughs burned in iron wall-sockets, throwing their flickering light over the many laughing faces of the shipmen and the villagers who served them with mead and corn-wine, or carried in the great wooden platters laden with barley bread and fish, or tender sucking pigs.

The smoke of the fire in the middle of the hall blew back in gusts from the high chimney-hole, for the wind was in a bad quarter. It was blowing out to the mouth of the fjord, and when that happened the smoke always seemed to come back, thick and choking, into the feast hall. But this night no one minded that, for all men spoke with great enthusiasm of the voyage they were about to make, no man knew where, in a great new ship as yet without a name.

Harald said to his father, 'It was a journey worth making, that through the forests, to reach such a place as this, and to be accepted among such men as these.' The boy's bright eyes lingered on the gay figure of Thorkell, who had dressed his beautiful hair with gold-braids for the feast and wore a sky-blue cloak that seemed to be woven of the very texture of summer.

Harald's father, Sigurd, curled his lip a little disdainfully. 'It is always thus, my son,' he said, 'before a voyage. Men seem heroes in the torchlight at a feasting.

But we must wait till the harsh salt cakes on their hands and the bitter wind tears their fine cloaks from them before we can judge whether they be true men or no.'

The boy gave a quick glance towards his father, an angry comment already forming on his lips. Then he thought the better of it and said nothing after all. Yet in that moment Harald hated his father a little for those slighting remarks about Thorkell Fairhair.

Seated next to Thorkell at the head of the long trestle table was the village headman, an old peasant with a fine leathern face, whose white hair hung down in snake-tails on either side of his head. He wore a thick frieze wrapper about his shoulders, for he was a sick man and the wind that blew down the valley at night-time brought on his rheumatism. Although a horn of corn-wine was set before him, he did not taste it, for he was an abstemious man who had never drunk anything but water from the springs, or at the best, goat's milk, when there was too much to be made into cheese. But this he did only infrequently, for he looked on such drinking as waste. A man might drink in five minutes enough milk to make a cheese that would last a family a week, he said to himself. This headman's name was Thorn. He was as sharp as his name. Although his hands were now too crippled to hold a stick, all the boys went in fear of him, and stopped whatever they were doing when he hobbled along the village street. It was this Thorn who had conceived the idea of building the longship and of sending it out to bring back treasure to the village. It was Thorn who had said, 'I choose Thorkell Fairhair for her master, if he should travel this way before we have finished her.' And all the villagers had agreed in their council, for every man liked Thorkell, and would trust their venture in his hands.

So it was that Thorn sat at Thorkell's side. And at last Thorn said, 'Master Thorkell, all goes well. The ship is ready and the crew chosen. If this wind holds, it will carry you out to sea tomorrow to begin your viking. But one thing is lacking. The ship has not been named, nor has she an emblem carved on her prow as most of our longships have. A raven or a dragon or a wolfhead.'

Thorkell smiled down at the old man lazily in the torchlight. 'Master Thorn,' he said, smiling, 'how call you this wine before the corn has been put into the mash-tub and wetted?'

All men listened as he spoke, some puzzled, some laughing. The old man blinked up at Thorkell, 'How call you it?' he said, wondering. 'How can we give it a name, for it is not yet made. It is nothing until the water is put on it and the corn has fermented. Nothing. It has no name.'

Thorkell said, 'What right has a man to call his sword "Brainbiter" until it has bitten a brain !'

The old man smiled tolerantly and said, 'We are talking of our ship – not of wine, or of swords, Thorkell.'

Thorkell said, 'Should a man name his ship "Land Ravager" if she is destined to sink before ever she sights land to ravage?'

When he said these words, many men crossed their fingers or spat upon the floor, to keep away the evil omens. 'He should not have said that,' whispered Aun Door-back, looking first over his right shoulder and then over his left, to see if the wicked ones were listening.

Thorkell sensed the unrest about the table at his words

and he laughed loud. 'My friends,' he said, 'we are fighting-men, not shivering old women, to be frightened with a strange word! I tell you that nothing ever happens unless it is fated to happen, long ago, before today or yesterday. Before last sowing or ten sowings before that. What happens was written down by Odin when the world was first made. It is there, in his writings, and nothing a man says can change it. Now, be still.'

'What then will you call the longship, Fairhair?' asked the old man, Thorn, impatiently. 'We built her and gave our money for her. We must know what her master will name her.'

At that moment Thorkell paused in his drinking and with a shrug of his broad shoulders stood up, so that all men watched him, wondering. Thorkell Fairhair pointed down the long table towards the Finn, Gnorre, who was at that moment hacking away with great concentration at his piece of salted beef. All men's eyes turned on the Finn, who looked back wide-eyed and surprised.

'Tell me your name, friend,' said Thorkell. 'I have forgotten it in the excitements of the day.'

The Finn said, 'Gnorre, Master. I am from Finland. I told you so earlier.'

Thorkell smiled again. 'By what other name are you known, Gnorre?'

Aun Doorback's face flushed and his great red hand began to fumble for his axe. But Gnorre patted him gently on the arm and whispered, 'Have patience, Aun. Perhaps he means well. You shall kill no more men for my sake. I can fend for myself, come the worst.'

Gnorre stood up, a strange bent figure in the torchlight, which played about his thin lined face. Then he spoke so proudly that all the hall was still and men listened.

'I am Gnorre Nithing, shipmaster,' he said. 'I took the knuckle-bones from you today as a viking, not as a prisoner to be handed back to those who would slay me for my past misdeeds. Now stand I here a warrior with a warrior's weapon and who takes me shall need to be a good swordsman.'

With that Gnorre leapt backwards with a speed that startled every man. And they saw that his sword, Grunter, was out and shining in the torchlight.

Then Aun Doorback had moved and the bench fell over, scattering the men who had been sitting at it among the rushes.

A woman screamed and one of the villagers dropped an earthen pitcher of wine. But Thorkell never moved a muscle. His gay face still smiled fixedly and his golden hair wafted softly in the breeze that stole in through the hide covering of the door.

Then he stretched out his hands towards Gnorre and Aun, almost in an attitude of pleading. 'I have picked two real men, my friends. I know a man when I see one, never fear. But when I asked your name it was so that everyone should see what I mean. Nothing more. All Finland must come to take you back, Gnorre, if they want you. But they must find their way beyond my sword guard to do it.'

Now Aun and Gnorre looked at each other like fools, a smile of embarrassment on their faces. The men who had fallen to the floor got up and scratched their heads, puzzled. The headman, Thorn, shook his grey head a little more, petulantly.

'Gnorre Nithing,' said Thorkell, 'you have given our ship her name. She shall be the *Nameless*. She shall wander as you have done, Gnorre, an outlaw of the seas. Perhaps all men's hands will be against her, as they are against you. But though she may be nothing at her launching, she may prove to be something at her beaching when she returns. Then we will give her another name, you and I.'

At first there was a hush in the long room, then everyone began to talk at once, and though the villagers did not seem to like the name, the shipmen were pleased with the way in which Thorkell had chosen it. For it seemed to free them of all responsibility. Now they would become outlaws, their own masters, to do as they pleased, obeying only their shipmaster, Thorkell.

Now men began to call to the villagers to fill up their wine-pannikins again, and here and there they began to slap each other on the back, sometimes a little too hard. And just when it seemed that the feast might become an excuse for rough horseplay among the vikings, Horic Laplander leapt on to the table, a weird misshapen figure in his bundled clothes, with his thick pigtail flying out behind him.

Now he whirled about in a strange winter dance of his people, striking grotesque attitudes, of bear or wolf and even of a pine tree. His padding feet now grew as noiseless as those of a mouse and he danced hither and thither among the drinking-horns and dishes without disturbing a thing. The men of the village, whose own dance was a heavy-footed stamping affair, gazed open-mouthed at his skill.

Then even Horic appeared to tire. He sank down in the

middle of the table and seemed to roll himself into a great ball. In this position he stayed still for such a space as a man might need to count twenty. Then without warning he sprang into life again, his hands held upwards and outwards, his feet wide apart and his thick body swaying. No man understood the language he spoke, for it was of the farthest northern forests and not spoken along the fjords for many hundreds of years. But they knew that Horic was telling them a story – a grim tale of the great forests and the wolves and the bears, and, worse still, of the old gods who demanded sacrifices in return for a good harvest, or a good reindeer foaling, or a good catch of fish. And they shuddered as they heard the gods speak through Horic's mouth, heard the forests sigh in his deep breathing, heard the wolves howl about the winter stockades, or the bears grunting outside the doors when all else was still and the children were asleep.

Now no one drank any more, or bothered to eat, though they still held their bread in their hands. Many even lost all knowledge of where they were, for the man's spell was so strong.

And then, when all stared at the Laplander, and even the torches set along the walls had stopped flickering, there came a great laugh from the darkness outside, and a moment later the hide covering at the doorway was flung aside with a single rough movement. The men in the hall turned slowly round, bemused, to see who had come, and then the spell was broken and Horic was no more than a little Laplander squatting on the table. The one who stood in the doorway had broken the magic, like an earthenware pot, it seemed.

Immensely tall and swarthy-faced, his raven hair hang-

ing below his dark and burnished helmet, the newcomer stood, his long black cloak reaching down to the straw on the floor. Men saw that his strong arms were bound about with ring after ring of gold. They saw the deep tattoo marks across his forehead and cheekbones, the oiled beard and the curling moustaches. This was a fine man, thought those who did not know him. This is an evil omen, thought those who did.

Thorkell gave a little gasp, 'Ragnar,' he said. 'Ragnar Raven ! I thought not to see you ever again !'

Ragnar smiled, a soft, dangerous smile, showing his white teeth. 'Do you mean "thought not" or "wished not," Thorkell Fairhair?'

Thorkell's face stiffened slightly and a cold air blew in through the open doorway from the fjord. He stepped forward.

'Enter and sit at the table-top, Ragnar,' he said. 'We are blood-brothers and come what may you shall share my fortune.'

Men moved away to let the proud stranger sit beside their leader.

Chapter 5 *The Blood-Launching*

The *Nameless* still stood on her stocks, above the runway of planks that led down to the waters of the fjord. With the arrival of Ragnar Raven the wind had changed and blew across the sea-inlet towards the village, so that it would have been madness to push the longship out only to have her dashed on the rocks that lay below the launching-place.

Men began to whisper, their heads together, saying that Ragnar had brought the venture ill-luck. Some men even said that, were it not that they loved Thorkell, they would have handed back the knuckle-bones and have gone on free up the fjord to find another ship.

Harald and his father kept together, for they were from inland and knew none of the others, the seafarers. Harald said to his father, 'I am afraid that this delay will spoil the crew.' Sigurd laughed and said, 'Sailors always grumble. Once they feel the planks bucking under their feet and get the sound of the sea-mews in their ears, they will forget all this. A viking is born, my son, and never escapes his destiny. As some men love horses, and others love hunting wolves, so a viking loves ships, every plank and rope of them, and he is never happy unless he is riding the track of the whale, treading the path of the gannet.'

Harald said, 'All the same, this Ragnar makes me wonder whether the venture will turn out well.'

Sigurd said, 'You are a young fool to bother your head with such thoughts. Ragnar is but a man, though a strong one. He can only do what Odin will let him. And we can only do what Odin will let us. So what can you change with all your worrying? You are but an ant crawling on a hunter's boot. That boot may carry you a long distance and you will think that life is good to you. Or it may crush you, then you will know no more. If you are a sensible ant you will not worry your head to discover what makes the boot move, for it will not alter your condition.'

The boy scratched his head and looked puzzled. Then he walked away and watched the villagers loading the *Nameless* with its tackle and threading the stay ropes through the pulleys that should hoist the main-sail.

On his way back to join his father he came upon Horic Laplander, sitting under the lee of a rock and holding a short length of tarred twine. The man was smiling, his eyes half-closed, and rocking back and forth. Harald saw that there were four knots in the twine that the man fingered so lovingly.

He tapped the Laplander on the thick shoulder. 'What are you doing, friend?' he said curiously.

Horic came out of his trance and whispered hoarsely, 'This is a bad wind for it keeps us ashore, quarrelling. I have just asked for a good wind to blow, now I must untie it so that it may come down the fjord and carry us out to sea.'

With a deft movement of his yellow hands he slacked the knot and gave it a tug. Then he shut his eyes and rocked back and forth again. Harald stood amazed and wondering. The wind which had been blowing into his face, slapping it roughly as he stood, ceased suddenly, and for a moment there was a complete stillness. Harald looked round and saw that the smoke from the chimney-holes was going up straight. Then, as though a great door had been opened somewhere up the valley, a low roaring noise came, growing louder and louder. At first the smoke still eddied, then it flicked like a whip-lash and began to flurry. The pine-trees high on the hill-top gave a faint sigh, then they too bent under the blast and began their own roar.

Now the wind struck Harald at the side of the head, and the smoke swept into his eyes. From the huts a man shouted, 'Praise Odin, the viking's wind has come!' And everywhere the cry went up, 'The viking's wind has come!'

Now all was bustle in the village. The headman hobbled out and said, 'Odin is pleased with our venture and wishes you to begin without delay. He has sent you a good wind.'

Only Horic still smiled, inscrutably, his length of twine now twisting in his yellow fingers, his eyes half-shut and his face contemptuous.

Sigurd said, 'This is beyond my knowledge. All men know that there are land-breezes and sea-breezes and that they come at different times of the day. But this is no ordinary land-breeze to come at midday, after three days of the other. I cannot understand it.'

Harald said, 'I am happier than I was, Father. If Horic sails there is one whose magic will put a check on Ragnar.'

Sigurd looked at his son, wondering, then said, 'Go into the feast hall, son, and eat well. You seem a little light-headed with hunger. Anyway, it is no bad thing to sail on a full stomach. Perhaps you will not want to eat for a day or two after we get started.'

Harald ate with the others while the villagers piled the provisions for the voyage near the shore – oat-cake, barley bread, salt-beef, pork and herring. Three large casks of fresh spring water stood among the other things, the most important of them all.

An hour later, Thorkell and Ragnar came out of the headman's hut, followed by Wolf, who now seemed crestfallen at having been replaced in his leader's affection. The headman was arguing loudly with them. He was saying, 'But Thorkell, you have a full crew. Your friend Ragnar has no place in the ship and you know it. He is an extra man and we all know that the gods do not like an extra man.'

Ragnar spat towards the fjord and said, 'Old wives' tales!'

This angered the headman. His hands began to shake violently and his daughter had to support him or he would have fallen on to the pebbles in his rage.

Thorkell patted him on the shoulder gently. 'Do not

frighten yourself, Thorn,' he said. 'Ragnar once saved my life and I owe him that. Now he goes where I go, if he chooses; and this time he does choose. We can say no more.'

Suddenly Ragnar turned on the headman and said, 'If that is all you are worrying about, an extra man, we can arrange that, old man. Under the old law a launching demands a blood sacrifice. Surely there is one among the crew who would lay his head upon the slipway to fulfil the ancient command?'

The headman glared up at him, speechless for a moment. Then he said, 'This village is a peaceful place. We do not sacrifice in the forest temples as they do in some parts. We are a free folk here and have been so since we formed our village settlement. Let who will pray to the gods of blood, we will not. Sooner than our ship went down the slipway through blood, I would burn her. She is ours, to do with as we please, and no one, not even Thorkell, shall tell us what we must do.'

Ragnar shrugged his shoulders and began to walk away whistling. Thorkell stared after him in anger for a moment, then helped the old man to his seat on the shore, near the slipway.

By the early afternoon all was ready for the launching. The crew stood on either side of the longship, resting their hands against the strakes, waiting to take the strain when Björn and his men had knocked away the supports with their great mallets. Then the vikings would push their ship down the runway into the water. Only Rolf Wryneck was aboard, holding his steerboard loosely, waiting to act when the ship was afloat, his thin neck twisted round and his sea-blue eyes misty as he gazed towards the bluer waters of the fjord.

Harald stood just beside his father, who was the first man at the bow of the ship, on the steerboard side. 'May she float well,' he prayed, his eyes half-closed. His father smiled and said, 'Never fear, son, she will. The men who made her might make one worthy of Odin !'

Hasting heard this and sucked in his breath loudly. 'That was a foolish thing to say, Sigurd,' he said. 'That is tempting Odin to make her sink.'

'On my own head be it,' said Sigurd, who was not a superstitious man. Then the last prop was knocked away, and Thorkell shouted, 'Vikings, take the strain – steady her – now heave !'

As he called out the last word, every shoulder was bunched, every arm tensed, all muscles strained. And when men thought that the longship would never move, she began to slide forward like a living thing.

But Sigurd let her go a little too late, and as she thrust forward, he lost his balance and toppled sideways in her tracks. Harald saw it happen and opened his mouth to shout, but he could not save his father. Then the vikings on the steerboard side saw Sigurd twist sideways and roll from the slipway, and many thought that he had come away unhurt. But those who dared to look saw that his rolling had been a little too late. All heard the bone of his leg breaking, and the man's stifled gasp. Then the *Nameless* slid smoothly down the slipway to the water.

Harald bent over his father, holding back the tears that burned his eyes. Yet even in his anguish he heard Ragnar's voice, 'I said that the old laws demanded a blood-launching, old man. Well, we have one now – and no extra man in the crew!' There was sardonic laughter in his voice. Harald shook the spurting tears from his eyes and tried to lift his father's body.

Sigurd opened his eyes and smiled grimly. 'I am not ready for Valhalla yet, lad,' he said. 'A broken leg mends easily with care, and if it doesn't, why, I have another leg!'

When he had said this, Sigurd fainted with pain. Thorkell patted Harald on the back and said, 'You have a brave father, boy. Let us hope his son is as much a viking.'

The headman had Sigurd carried into his own hut, to be tended by his daughter. Then all the crew clustered on the shore, as though nothing had happened worth noticing, for the *Nameless* was riding the rough fjord waters like a swan, graceful and strong. The vikings sent up a great cheer and some of the villagers began their uncouth dance on the shore, relieved that their vessel had not let them down.

At last Harald made his way to the headman's hut.

His father was sleeping, but the headman's daughter said, 'He will be well again, one day, never fear. We shall care for him. He commands that you go on your voyage as though he were with you.'

'But I cannot leave him,' said Harald.

'Is the son less of a viking than the father?' asked the girl.

Harald stood ashamed. The girl smiled at him then and said, 'This is his home now, as it is yours when you are not voyaging. Come and say good-bye to your father before you sail, that is all. Now go and get your things together, for Thorkell will not be pleased with you if you lag behind at the sailing.'

Harald went out of the hut. Men were loading the provisions aboard, and the vikings were already choosing their places in the ship, and packing their few belongings into the sea-chests on which they sat to row. Here and there along the side of the *Nameless*, men were hanging their shields, one overlapping the other, to keep the water out in a high sea.

Harald stood irresolute for a moment, then suddenly he felt that he must ask Odin to look after his father while he was away from him. An idea struck him and without looking back at the ship, he turned and ran as hard as he could up the hill-side towards the great forest.

At last, tired and panting, he stood on the outskirts of the wooded heights. Choosing the greatest pine he could see, he slipped off his gold arm-ring and flung it up into the boughs, saying, 'An offering, Father Odin. It is all I have to give you. May my father prosper and be made whole again.'

Then he turned to go down to the ship again. But as he went he began to recall how he had rejoiced when his father had come striding towards Gudröd's Hall, laughing and bearing that same gold ring.

'Wear this, my son,' he had said. 'And may fortune smile upon us all the days it clasps your arm.'

Now he had thrown away his father's precious gift. Suddenly it did not seem the right thing to do. Moreover, his father had prayed for success to fall upon *them*, not him alone. As he stood under the great pine-tree, Harald, his dark northern superstitions stifling his reason, feared that by giving away the ring, even to Odin, he was some-how working against, and not for, his father's chances of survival.

With a low cry, he began to climb the pine-tree. It was not easy. Nor was the ring at first visible. But at last he saw it, dangling precariously, between two small shoots. Ignoring the difficulties, and the pain of the ascent, he clambered up towards it. And, as he reached out to take it, he begged Odin to forgive him.

'One day, I will make you a finer offering, Father,' he said. He put the ring back upon his arm. And then he froze in a sudden fear. He heard voices below the tree. And one voice that he already knew. He looked down cautiously. Three men stood at the edge of the wood, only a few yards beneath him, talking earnestly and smiling wickedly. One of them was Ragnar. The others were not of the venture and Harald did not recognize them. Yet he saw by their ornaments and their black hair that they must be of Ragnar's own folk, Danes.

Ragnar was saying, 'So, my friends, this is your chance. Ride fast and tell them up the fjord that we sail today. Yours is a bigger ship and should find us before we are far from shore. Have no fear, Thorkell will do as I wish.'

One of the others said, 'Then perhaps we can take the *Nameless* without having to fight?'

Ragnar turned on him with a black scowl. 'Not even I can make Thorkell lay down his arms. No, he will fight, whatever happens. I meant that I can cause him to furl sail if it seems that we have too great a start on you, so that you may catch up. And don't forget, I shall have to make a pretence at fighting by his side. See that your men know that. I do not want them to come at me like boars, or they will take an arm from me by mistake !'

Harald said grimly to himself, 'An arm for a leg, Ragnar ! You deserve it !' Then the tears flooded his eyes again and blinded him. When he looked again they had gone, and Ragnar was striding down the hill towards the longship, waving to Thorkell.

Harald followed after him at a distance, wondering what he could do to prevent Ragnar's treachery. One thing he dared not do and that was tell Thorkell about it yet, for there was no proof. Whatever he did must be done when they were well afloat.

Harald stopped at the headman's hut. His father greeted him warmly and kissed him on both cheeks. 'Go, my young viking,' he said. 'And may Odin heal my leg well enough for me to follow you on the next ship that sails from this fjord. Now go, and all fortune with you. If you stay longer I shall forget that I am a warrior.'

But Harald was not yet a warrior. The tears ran down his cheeks unchecked as he clambered into the *Nameless*.

The *Nameless* moved slowly away from the shore, heading towards the open sea which lay not much more than ten miles away. Harald stood beneath the mast, looking up at those of the villagers who ran alongside, on the rocks above the fjord, keeping up with the ship for as long as they might, and shouting down messages of good-will to the crew. Then his eyes filled with tears and he lowered his head.

When he looked up again, the village on the shore was out of sight. The great adventure had started. Now Harald's heart lifted and he began to think more calmly about his father's misfortunes. He consoled himself by thinking that Odin had wished it to happen as it did. And Sigurd would be the first to agree with that, Harald felt sure, after what he had said earlier.

Now Harald looked about him in the longship. The oarsmen seated on their sea-chests had stopped rowing, for the wind had freshened enough to carry them well away from the rocky shore and out in the middle of the fjord. The great coloured sail was unfurled, and bellied out strongly, proudly displaying its bright coloured stripes. The white pennant stuck out almost rigid, towards the bow of the boat, in the following breeze.

Harald sat down, over the loose planks in the middle of the ship, below which the provisions and weapons were stored, the latter oiled with pig's fat and wrapped in sheepskin to keep them dry. Beside him sat four others, playing dice and telling tales already. There were sixteen oar-ports on each side of the *Nameless*, which meant that she needed thirty-two oarsmen to keep her going well. Thorkell as the leader, and Rolf as the steersman, stood in the stern. Ragnar, self-appointed as second-in-command, stood in the bow, acting as a look-out. So were the forty shipmen disposed in the *Nameless*. The five who rested replaced oarsmen as they became tired, and were themselves later replaced by others who had enjoyed a spell away from the oars. Though, once out in the open sea, it was not the custom to use oar-power – and then the men rested, waiting for the first sight of land.

Overhead the afternoon sky was clear and blue in the sun's light. The white gulls swept here and there about the ship, sometimes just skimming the mast-top, as though they were curious about this new creature that had come to ride the waves with them. One gull even alighted on the high golden prow, just above Ragnar's head, and seemed to regard him for a while, critically, before flying away to its fellows with a harsh squawk. At this, many of the vikings smiled, and one or two of them even laughed aloud.

'A gull can judge a man,' whispered Björn to Hasting, for neither of them had any love for this arrogant newcomer to the crew.

Hasting said, 'He holds the place that you should have by rights, my friend. You built this ship and none knows her better than you.'

'That's as may be,' said Björn, who was a reasonable man. 'If Thorkell says that Ragnar is to be second-master of her, who am I to deny it?' And he went on whittling at a piece of oak which he had brought with him on to the ship. The oak-chips lay about his feet, gold in the sunlight, until the wind whipped them away and over the side of the *Nameless*.

At length Rolf Wryneck called out to Harald, telling him to come and try his hand at steering. The boy forgot his lingering sadness, in face of this high honour, and moved over the gently swaying deck. As he passed along the shipside, the men he knew called out to him, smiling and patting him on the back, to keep his courage up. Aun Doorback pulled him aside and said, 'Your father is a fine man, lad. And with strong arms like these of yours, you will do him justice on this voyage.'

Harald went on along the deck feeling pleased at the big man's words. Rolf Wryneck said, 'Watch me for a few minutes, lad, and then see how you can hold her.'

Harald did as he was told, and then took the long horn-shaped haft. The ship was now his, his to command and steer. He felt the steerboard shudder, then pull away from him, and, when he had used all his strength on the haft, felt it strike a course and hold it. He had the illusion that the ship was a living thing, like a horse, and that for a moment he had mastered it. Rolf was watching him, a bright light in his eyes. He smiled to see Harald's new confidence and said, 'Ships be like any other creature. Show them who is master and they will obey; but once let them have the upper hand and they will run wild and break their backs in rebellion.'

Thorkell had watched all this, and laughed to hear Rolf's words.

'Does she ride well, you old gossip?' he asked Rolf.

Rolf shook his head, in his strange twisted way, and

grinned, 'Aye, Master,' he said. 'She rides smoother than any ship I have ever held except the *Gullchaser* that I made my first voyage in.'

Thorkell saw the reminiscent gleam in the man's eye. 'What became of her?' he asked.

Harald saw that Rolf's eyes were wet now. 'She tried to leap a rock off the Northumbrian coast, Master,' he said. 'I was the only one to come away from her, and sometimes I wish I had stayed with my fellows. I have this twisted neck to remember that rock by. Some say I broke it that day, and that it never set right.'

'Odin is keeping you for greater things,' said Thorkell. Suddenly Harald felt his tongue unlocked and he dared to speak. 'Shipmaster,' he said, 'there is something which weighs on my mind. I would tell you of it.'

Thorkell smiled down at him. 'If you wish to ask for Rolf's job, save yourself the trouble. Rolf steers very well for my purposes.' Harald would not be put off now by such jesting. 'Shipmaster,' he said, 'I fear there is treachery aboard, to rob us of the *Nameless*. I heard men talking in the woods. Ragnar's men.'

Thorkell's eyes narrowed and his lean jaws twitched. He glanced over his shoulder and then said, almost in a whisper. 'Tell me no more, boy. A little bird has already whispered to me about something.'

He saw the boy's wide-eyed incredulity, and patted him on the arm, saying, 'When you become a shipmaster, you develop eyes in the back of your head. And even the gulls bring messages to the man who can understand them.'

Then he went amidships, without another word, leaving Harald staring after him, dumbfounded, and knelt down by Horic, who was sitting away from the other vikings, looping and unlooping his length of twine and mumbling to himself.

Harald wondered at this. It seemed that Thorkell wished to speak secretly with the Laplander, for no man could hear the words he spoke. But then Harald saw Horic rise and point back the way they had come, and then nod his head violently at something which Thorkell had said. After that, Thorkell came back and stood near the steerboard, but now with a distant, abstracted air, as though there were weighty things on his mind. He was a man who had more to work out than his years would let him do easily, it seemed. Rolf, who was wise in the ways of men, put his strong sinewy hand on Harald's arm, and nodded in the direction of their shipmaster, as though to say, 'Keep out of his way for the moment. Something troubles him, and a man who is troubled in his mind might bite and do hurt without intending it.' So the boy watched carefully, but did not think to speak with his leader as he had done but a little earlier.

In fact, none of the men spoke to Thorkell. He stood, chin in hand, his back against the ladder that led up to the platform at the stern of the longship, his eyes dark and foreboding. Even Ragnar, the arrogant Ragnar of but a few hours before, glanced back a time or two, and then decided not to disturb the young warrior's thoughts.

At length the afternoon gave place to early evening, and as it was springtime, the dusk came on quite soon afterwards. Now the air became sharper and a salt tang came to the nostrils of the vikings. The sea was not far away. Now the birds that circled the mast-head were not gulls alone, but also those feathered inhabitants of the deep-sea rocks, the cormorant and the shag, flying who knows whither? Carrying the spirits of drowned seamen who knows where? The vikings looked upwards and shook their heads with foreboding.

Once a goshawk, from the woods high on the hills that overlooked the widening fjord, poised high above them and seemed to set the pennant of the *Nameless* in its cruel eye, as though to swoop down. Then it decided that this was not its true prey, and swept away from the scene in a broad swoop of wings, away, away, towards the dusky forests.

Then Harald noticed something unusual about Thorkell. The young man was listening, listening, not seeing, for sight over any distance was impossible now. It was as though he was listening to the wake that his ship made; listening even beyond that wake; beyond the village from which they had started that day. . . .

And suddenly he made a sign to Horic, who crouched beside him looking up.

Harald looked towards Ragnar, almost instinctively. The tall Dane was listening too. His white hands were clenched hard on the gunwale nearest to him, his body was tense. Every muscle in his dark body seemed to be waiting for something.

The men playing dice or yarning together did not notice these things. They only smelt the salt in the air and heard the different cries of the deep-sea birds. They only heard Thorkell's voice, a new and urgent voice that they did not know, shout out, 'Steersman, set course to shore. There we shall spend our first night's voyaging.'

Some of the men sighed with relief as the *Nameless* pulled into the shore and they knew that they would not spend their first night fighting the rolling waves that swung down from Iceland towards the Pillars of Hercules.

So the longship beached in the dusk, less than five miles from where it was launched. Those who wished slept aboard, for a long tarred cloth was stretched over the centre-posts that stood one on each side of the mast. Those who wished went ashore and slept in their sheepskin bags, under rock or bush. Though they were not allowed to make a fire, by Thorkell's strict orders; no man knew why.

That night Thorkell said to Harald, 'Boy, your father broke a limb serving me. Under our law I am now your father, being your accepted leader. That is my obligation. Until you can fend for yourself, you are my son. You will sleep near me and do as I say.'

Harald secretly laughed at the idea of having a father so young as Thorkell; yet in his innermost heart he was proud that this warrior should take him as son. He bowed his head in acknowledgement and got into his sleepingbag at Thorkell's feet.

Then Harald fell fast asleep, without another thought of the ship, or the voyage, or Thorkell, or Ragnar, or Horic – or even of his dear father, five miles along that same shore, lying in the hut of the kindly headman, Thorn.

When he woke, a chill air blew about him. Even the woods above him were still, as though the birds were not yet sure of themselves. He looked across at Thorkell, who was awake and staring out towards the fjord. Harald followed his gaze and saw that the waters were now leaden, and still ruffled, as though a great storm had swept them in the night and had not yet died down.

Thorkell said, 'Make ready, boy, for I shall not wait long here.'

Then Harald went aboard again, but noticed that Thorkell was walking with Horic, and that Ragnar was behind them, pulling at his beard with anger.

The longship sailed again before the vikings had fed. They ate what they could aboard as the dawn came slowly across the sky behind them. Some ate of oatmeal, soaked in fresh water, others of barley bread, and yet others, the hardiest of the voyagers, of dried fish. This was a meal to turn the squeamish stomach, for the herring were strong in smell and taste, and might not be enjoyed by any but the toughened traveller.

Soon the *Nameless* began to rock. Harald looked ahead and saw great foam-headed breakers. They were approaching the sea – that vast world which the poets had called 'the gulls' way,' 'the whales' way,' 'the track of the dolphin,' and other fanciful titles. To Harald it was something new and different and frightening. A young viking among vikings, he was, in his heart, afraid. Though he would have lost an ear rather than admit it. The sea was before him. The deep, salt sea !

Now the sailors put out their oars and helped the sail to do its work, and Harald heard many words spoken that he had not heard before, for these men knew what it was to fight an incoming tide. They knew how a tide will first warm, then blister, then crack the skin of their hands; will bend the back and then bring it nigh unto breaking. These were old vikings, who knew the sea as a friend, an enemy, a grave.

Then at last, when the ship was moving smoothly again and the breakers were less noticeable, Harald looked back and saw the rocky headlands and the high forests only distantly. He knew that they were now truly a-voyaging!

Some of the men had gone back to sleep, even the oarsmen, their blades pulled up and safe against the rollers. Even Ragnar, at the bow, resting his great dark head down on the gunwale. . . .

Then Harald woke with a start. Thorkell's voice said, 'Care, take care to steerboard, watch for the wreck!'

All men looked where he pointed. On the surging waves rested the remains of a longship. She rolled carelessly with the tide, a neglected thing, her bright planks ignored by all but the sea-birds that already sat upon her, gossiping. What had been her sail, a white sail marked with a black raven, floated in bellying ripples about her. Her oars jostled each other about her sides, for she lay turtle-wise, her loose keel uppermost.

A great gasp ran along the *Nameless*. This was the end all sailormen feared – dreamed of, and feared. Now men clustered along the gunwales to see what there was to see.

A covey of gulls swung about and about the wrecked longship.

'Something must be living here,' said Björn, who knew every mood of the sea and of its birds.

Thorkell said, 'Head towards the wreck, Rolf.'

The *Nameless* shuddered like a shot goose as she turned her golden prow to where the sea-birds were quarrelling.

Aun said, 'Odin save us from such an end, Gnorre.'

Gnorre hung on his oar and did not speak.

Harald, curious, thought he saw a hand raised, and dark hair floating with the tide. For some nights after,

he even thought he heard a hoarse voice screaming for help. But he was not sure. All he knew was that Thorkell shouted, 'Ease away, Rolf. A viking clings to the spars. Alongside and get him aboard.'

Then Harald saw Ragnar unhook the long seal-spike that hung beside him at the forward end, and lean over the bows, looking intently into the sea.

Gnorre, who stood as he rowed, said, 'He means to save the man.'

Aun, standing beside him, said, 'Who knows?'

Then the *Nameless* swept past the wreckage and Ragnar turned back with a shrug of the shoulders, and a grim smile towards Thorkell.

Harald ran to the steerboard side but could see no man. 'Hold course,' called Thorkell, with a sigh.

Horic whispered to himself, but every man near him heard, 'Look, there is blood upon the point of Ragnar's seal-spike.'

When the vikings turned to look, Ragnar took the long harpoon and held it in the sea, so that the running waves covered it.

'I have known men take a fish or two this way,' he said with a smile, to the oarsman who sat nearest him.

Wolf Waterhater, his red hair wet with sweat, did not smile back at him.

Chapter *7 The Gulls' Way*

From the day when the *Nameless* had run upon the wreckage, many of the vikings hated Ragnar. For, like all true seamen, the voyagers both loved and hated the sea, but above all regarded her as a constant danger; and they felt bound in a strange way to give aid to all who suffered by the sea, even though the sufferers were men whose ships they had themselves wrecked in a sea-fight. Against the merciless waves, all vikings were brothers, save in the most extreme cases when, by giving help to the wrecked, they might endanger the safety of their own longship.

Yet, among all voyagers there were those with the hearts of wolves, who gave no quarter to any man. These were the fierce brutes who sailed down upon holy places and burned and pillaged without compassion. Ragnar was such a man.

But as the *Nameless* pushed on across the northern sea, the vikings had other things to occupy their minds. When they had muttered to each other for a while, they forgot the wreck and turned to their task of bracing the sail, or rowing when the winds lagged. Once they had to take buckets and bail feverishly when they struck a patch of water that rose above them like the foothills above the village they had left. Harald, seeing the great waters rising high above him, wanted to cry out in fear, for it seemed that they would topple down upon the frail shell in which he sailed, to crush everything into oblivion. He could not see how any craft might survive such a smashing blow. But though he was terrified, there was nowhere he might run, to escape the fury of the salt waters. He stood rooted and would undoubtedly have been swept overboard had not Gnorre pushed a rope into his hands and yelled in his ear, 'Grasp this for your life! The sea does not play bower-games!' Harald saw that all the others were clutching tight to anything that might be at hand. Even proud Ragnar held the ladder near the forward platform, his head bent as though he wished to evade the full force of the blow.

Then the green mountain of water crashed down upon them and for a while Harald only knew that a rushing, roaring nightmare had enveloped him. He heard nothing but the sound of great waters; he tasted nothing but bitter brine; and he was drenched through and through, as though the sea had penetrated to his innermost heart.

At last he shook the water from his eyes and ears and was able to look about him. The oarsmen were lying sprawled in the lee of their sea-chests. Only Thorkell and Rolf stood erect, and both were smiling. It was that strange smile which put new heart into Harald, and he tried to smile too. Thorkell saw the boy's grin and beckoned him to come aft. 'That was but the pat of a bear-cub,' he said to the boy. 'When we face the big seas beyond the islands, you will feel the weight of the grown bear's paw!'

Now the sun came out and the *Nameless* ran into clearer waters. The men took off their leather tunics and rubbed each others' backs with rough cloths, to get warmth into their bodies again. It was then that Harald saw Aun's back for the first time without its rough covering of bear-hide. It seemed to the boy that the breadth of his back was almost as great as the span of a child's arms, held outstretched. But what most interested Harald was the great blue dragon that was tattooed there, its head between his shoulder-blades, its tail disappearing somewhere into the rough leathern breeches that he wore.

It was with something of a shock that Harald saw Gnorre's back, for it was so thin and bunched, and worse still, it was covered with white weals, criss-crossed in many directions, the marks of a vicious whip. It seemed that Gnorre Nithing had not escaped unhurt from the land where he had killed a man. Harald felt very sorry for him, but wondered how such a man could possibly be the warrior men thought. For Harald had little experience of men and expected all fighting-men to be cast in the same mould, that of a godlike hero, a Thorkell, or even a Ragnar.

Later, when the shipmaster had sanctioned an issue of the warming corn-wine that was kept in stone bottles under the planking amid-ships, the vikings let the mainsail do all the work, while they sat round in the sun, talking and singing. Rolf sang a song which they all seemed to know, for they joined in the chorus, thumping out the rhythm with their fists on the planks beside them. To Harald it was all new and he listened, wide-eyed, his mouth half-open, to the tale it told.

It was the story of a hunter who slept in a cave one winter's night, warm and contented, only to find in the morning that the heap of skins on which he had rested was a sleeping bear, drowsy with hibernation. When the song came to the point where the hunter put out his hand and felt the animal's wet muzzle, Harald gave a little gasp, and Wolf Waterhater slapped him on the back and said that he had once done the same, only the creature turned out to be a whale. Harald told him not to be so stupid, for whales didn't live in caves. Wolf said quite solemnly, 'Oh, this was a cave under the sea. As a matter of fact, it upset me so much that I have avoided water ever since.'

The rough men about Harald laughed at the lad's expression, for although he had been taken in by Wolf's serious expression at first, he knew that he was being teased and felt angry that Wolf should imagine he would believe such nonsense.

Then Wolf pretended that Harald meant to strike him, so still sitting, he clasped the lad round the waist and began to wrestle with him. Then, when he had tired of this, Wolf slung the lad over to Aun, who ruffled his hair and poked him in the ribs playfully – though hard enough to make Harald gasp – and so passed him round to Gnorre, who let him get up after giving him a slap. Yet it was all done with good humour, and Harald's expression of annoyance at Wolf's yarn had soon passed away.

Horic, who had watched the horse-play, said solemnly, 'That is good advice, Harald. When you are angry, go and wrestle with your friends. It will bring smiles back to your heart and you will forget your anger.'

Aun said, 'What do you know of wrestling, little monkey?' He looked so fierce as he spoke that Harald thought a quarrel was about to begin, but the others laughed. Then Horic, still smiling, leaned over and grasped Aun's thick wrist and slowly twisted it until the great man lay face downwards on the boards. And when Aun had beaten with his other hand three times, to signify that he would give in, Horic let him rise again, rubbing his wrist as though it hurt, but smiling now.

'You see,' said Horic, 'Aun was angry. Now he is glad.'

'Yes, glad you let me get up again,' said Aun. 'But never fear, monkey, I will get the better of you one day.'

'Perhaps when I am asleep,' said Horic. 'Or better still, when you are asleep, and dreaming!'

It was during these early days of the voyage that Harald learned of the many proverbs with which Norsemen sprinkled their talk. One of them that stuck in his mind went: 'Praise no day till evening, no sword until tested, no ice until crossed, and no ale until it has been drunk.' This was a saying which reflected the viking's cautious approach to many things in life. Yet there was another side to the Norse character that was also shown in the tales they told each other. It was a love of exaggeration that made them roar with laughter when it figured in a tale they were listening to.

For instance, there was the story of the brothers, to whom bad news was brought; one of them grasped his spear-shaft so tightly that the imprint of his fingers bit deep into the hard wood; another was playing chess, and crumbled the ivory chessman to pieces as he gripped it; the third was cutting his fingernails and sliced his finger down to the bone without noticing it, such was his rage.

As these tales were told, the men of the *Nameless* howled with glee at each succeeding exaggeration, and even vied with each other to make up still more impossible incidents.

Yet, despite this fanciful yarning, when it came to their own experiences, they were tight-lipped and dour, for to be called a boaster was considered worse than being called a thief. To be called a murderer, of course, meant hardly anything at all, since it depended on whether the man one had murdered had a weapon in his hand. If he had, then no man thought more of the incident.

Harald learned much about his fellow Northmen in the three days they spent in crossing the northern sea. But he learned little more of Ragnar, or even of Thorkell, for now they kept themselves away from the others and spent much time under the platform aft, talking quietly.

Björn said to Hasting, 'Yon Thorkell must make the best of a bad bargain, I fear.'

Hasting replied with a wry smile, 'I think he has bitten off more than he can chew, bringing Ragnar aboard.'

But Kragge, who was passing at the time, stopped and looked down on them sourly. 'Let not your tongues wag too fast, my friends,' he said. 'This Ragnar may well be a better man to follow than Thorkell. I have watched him closely these two days and he seems to be a man's man, even if a maid may not like his face so well as the golden-haired lad's.'

Björn, who respected Thorkell and hated Ragnar, said, 'You are a fool, Kragge. Are there any more fools aboard this ship like you?'

Kragge made a gesture of the thumb behind him. 'Gryffi and Ivar, and a dozen others, think the same,' he said. 'We are not voyaging for our health, my friend. We come for treasure, and we count that leader a good one who takes us to where treasure may be found.'

Björn looked back at him with dislike, but said, 'How do you know that this Ragnar will lead you to treasure?'

Kragge said, 'I know the sort of man he is. I was farthest forward when he took the seal-spike and rode beside the wreck. There was a man there, clinging to a spar. And that man knew Ragnar, for I heard him call on him by name. You others could not hear that for the pounding of the waters on the ship's sides. But I heard it. And I saw what Ragnar did with the harpoon he held.'

Hasting said, 'Go back to your friends, Kragge, for you are a fool to follow such a man.'

But Kragge said, 'And you are a child, Hasting, not to see that this Ragnar, being so ruthless, is such a leader as would stop at nothing once his mind was set towards a thing. He is the man to bring us to our hearts' desire. He is a man to be followed.'

'Aye, and feared,' said Björn, turning his head in disgust.

'Who thinks worse of a man for that?' said Kragge. 'That is what a leader should be, for if we fear him it means that our enemies must surely fear him more!'

He went back to his fellows at Ragnar's part of the ship and soon seemed to be telling them what had passed.

Hasting said, 'I have seen this happen before, and often it means that a ship does not return, for when the crew divide, the ship becomes her own master, and then breaks her sides on the teeth of the rocks.'

Björn said, 'Perhaps it is not as bad as we think. Perhaps we shall become a crew again when we sight land. It is this sea-crossing that upsets a man's mind. It comes hard, even to a viking, after a winter spent on the sheepskins by a hall fire.'

Harald was lying close to them when this happened, his head pillowed on a coil of rope. He heard it all without meaning to. When the men had finished speaking he went to Björn and told him that he had heard. 'Well, then, boy, you have heard, that is all,' said Björn. 'Which captain would you follow?'

Harald said, 'I gave my word to Thorkell, and him will I follow through thick and thin, wet and dry, sun and shower.'

Hasting said, 'You are a true Norseman, lad, like your father, Sigurd. One day, if sea and rock will let you, you will grow to be a viking.'

Then Aun, who had been sent to act as look-out, called through his cupped hands, 'Land ahoy! Land on the starboard!'

Harald ran towards Aun and stared in the direction of his pointing finger. A thin blue-grey haze seemed to rest on the surface of the waters, far away. Then it would disappear and Harald would wonder whether his eyes had played him tricks; whether indeed that haze existed at all. Then, when he had rubbed his eyes and had come to the conclusion that he had imagined it all, the haze would appear again, a fine ribbon, as distant and as flimsy as a dream.

Now all the vikings ran to the starboard side and peered under their hands. They knew what to look for and there was no doubt in their exclamations of surprise and joy.

Thorkell gave the order for all men to eat and drink their fill, for soon they would be able to replenish their stores, and in any case, if there was fighting to be done, it was best that it should be done on a full stomach, provided there was time enough for the meal to be digested, and, from the look of the land, he said, they would not beach for another two hours.

Chapter **8** *The First Prize*

It was at this point, when the seamen were sitting on the deck, knife and drinking-horn in hand, that Aun shouted out once more.

'A ship, a ship, lying in our course!'

This time Harald had no difficulty in seeing what had excited the great look-out man. Rising and falling with the surging tides was a small boat that carried a square sail. It was too far distant for him to see more, for the vessel looked no larger than a small seed rocking on the waters.

Now the men of the *Nameless* flung down their bread and their meat, and drank off their fresh water at a gulp. The deck-boards amidships were raised, the weapons distributed to their owners without delay. Once more Hasting caressed his axe, Dream-maker, and Rolf Wryneck his dagger, Battlefang. Only Horic was without a weapon, and, though he protested, Thorkell made him take a sword out of store, an unnamed rough-cast blade, meant for such an emergency.

'See that it does such work as to deserve a name to-night,' joked Wolf Waterhater. But Horic looked utterly lost, holding such a blade.

Now Thorkell became their leader again, wearing such an expression of severity on his youthful face that all men obeyed him without question.

He gathered the men about the platform at the stern,

and standing above them told them what they were to do. First, the sail was to be furled and taken down, and they were to row to within a distance such that the other vessel would not see their oars. Then they would pull in the oars and drift, each man hidden under the platforms, or lying close to the ship's sides, covered by skins or old clothes. On no account was any sound to be made. The *Nameless* was to appear deserted, as though the crew had abandoned her and she was left derelict.

All save Ragnar warmed to this stratagem. He only spoke up, saying, 'Why do we not sail right in and take her direct, without such mockery of battle?'

Thorkell smiled down on him and said, 'If this ship comes from the far coast, as I think she does, her ship-master would see us coming and would turn for his own shore, to reach haven long before we could hope to catch him. Then what sort of welcome would we receive, think you? A hornet's nest about the ears, and the end of a short voyage for us all!'

Some of the men, including Aun and Hasting, laughed and jeered at little at Ragnar, when this answer was made. But Kragge and Gryffi mumbled and muttered that Ragnar's was the right way of tackling the problem. At last this whispering faded, however, and all men did as they were bidden.

To Harald, lying half-stifled under a pile of sacking, the waiting was never-ending. He thought that surely night must have fallen before he heard voices, speaking in a language which he did not know. Then he heard Gnorre whisper to Aun, 'If this should be my day, I will take your greetings to your brother, though we were enemies in life.' Then he heard Aun say, 'I send him no greetings, brother. See that you stand back to back with me and we shall live to take a hundred more ships.'

There was a silence then, and Harald found that his teeth were chattering violently. Under the pile of sacking, he clutched tightly at the long spear that Thorkell had given him.

So tightly, in fact, that for a moment he wondered whether his fingers would leave their imprint in its shaft, like the one in the saga he had heard. This made him laugh at himself, and he began to understand how men went 'berserk.' He had never seen a Berserk, but he had heard many tales of them, for of all the vikings they were the most respected. They were men who tore off their shirts and ran half-naked into the fray, careless of life, trying to take as many men to Valhalla with them as they could. Strangely enough, they lived to see many battles, most of them, whereas the saner fighters lasted a much shorter time.

As he lay under his sacking, Harald recalled that his father had once said that a good average for any man was a round dozen of battles. After that the chance of survival became gradually smaller and smaller. His father had gone on to say that this didn't apply to a Berserk, for they were usually so drunk, one way or another, that they fell lightly and seemed to survive where a normal man would have broken his neck. He instanced one case where one Thor Baldhead, a notorious Berserk along the fjords, had fought with great distinction in eighty-five affrays, both great and small, in all places from Orkney to Byzantium. This Thor had once run amok in Frankland and had cut his way thirty yards into a solid phalanx of guards, until he reached the horse on which the King of the Franks sat, petrified. With a last sweep of his axe he had struck off the horse's head and was then borne down by the spear-points of a dozen guards and left for dead. At dawn the next day, when the old women were searching the field for treasures, one of them had trodden on his finger and wakened him. He jumped up, wounded all over his chest and arms, and they had thought he was a spirit and had run away.

Then Thor found a mail shirt belonging to one of the Frankish king's guards, and a helmet that one of the vikings had left lying about, and had walked all the way back to the coast, a distance of twenty miles, unmolested. A month later he was back in Norway, and ready to go a-viking once more. This Thor, said Harald's father, died at the age of forty-two, a great age for a viking, from an adder's bite when he happened to be trepassing in the garden of a Moorish Caliph in Spain. It was a sad end, thought his comrades, for the physician who treated him did not know of the viking hatred of dying in bed, and so poor Thor died a cow's death, with two Arab slaves holding him down as he tried to struggle to his feet.

All these things came to young Harald's mind as he lay under the sacking, listening to the voices of the strangers in their square-sailed boat.

Then he heard the grating of wood on wood, and knew that the ships lay alongside each other. Suddenly a whisper ran through the *Nameless* . . . and all men lay tense and sweating, grasping sword or mace or heavy axe.

Then the tumult broke loose; light came upon them all, either because they had flung off their covering, or because the boarding party had dragged the sacking and skins aside.

Now the deck of the *Nameless* was a swarming mass of men, thrusting and stabbing and slashing at each other.

Harald saw Gryffi go down, a spear through his breast. Then he saw Kragge standing over Ivar, his knife Home-getter darting here and there, and at each thrust drawing a howl or a curse.

Aun and Gnorre were by his side, back to back, scything great swathes of men before them. And now Harald saw that Gnorre was smiling and even singing, a long low rhythmic tune, which Aun caught up in the chorus, so that they both were singing aloud at the end. And at the end of each verse, a man fell, and another verse started.

Once a man fell at Harald's feet. His face was daubed with a blue paint, and his red hair was tied with bone pins. His eyes rolled horribly up at the boy and he seemed to be trying to get up and thrust with a long sword. Harald gripped his spear-shaft so hard that his hands became quite numb, and for the life of him he could not have stabbed down at his enemy. Then, as a thick haze seemed to drift across his eyes, a sword came out from behind him and the blue-painted man lay still. Harald turned, bewildered, to see Horic's bland smile. Then the boy realized that each of the vikings of the *Nameless* had paired up, and were standing back to back. Horic had silently chosen to be Harald's war-friend. The boy smiled back, feeling rather sick, and Horic grinned as he kissed the blade of his new sword. 'This Pict-pricker,' he said, solemnly.

It was at this stage of the fight that many men heard a curious and monotonous chanting from above. They looked up to see Thorkell, his golden mail-shirt discarded, his wild hair flying about his shoulders, his pale blue eyes full of an empty ecstasy. In his hand the sword whirled so rapidly that the sun seemed to create a new globe of light about him. Harald understood the man's secret then; he was a Berserk. That was why the others followed him.

Then Harald had his second shock. Ragnar was by Thorkell's side, stripped to the waist, his black head beside Thorkell's fair one, his great axe whirling in time with his friend's sword. And together they sang a song which must have been rehearsed in many such a fray as this, for no syllable fell out of place.

For a while, the fighting below seemed to eddy and still itself. Then, with a frightening scream, the two men leapt down.

Harald closed his eyes, feeling weak at the knees. He was angry with himself at feeling so, and at the same time half ready to call out for his father, as he used to do when a small boy. Then something else came into his heart; a man was but flesh and blood, after all, his brain said. What one can do, another may attempt! And now he stepped forward, his spear-shaft held loosely, his eye on the alert for an enemy.

But he was too late. The fight was over, and the *Nameless* looked very different from what it had been but four days before. The other vessel had put grappling hooks into the gunwales of the longship and so could not get away easily. What remained of her crew were huddled in the other boat. The vikings swarmed aboard her, led by Thorkell and Ragnar. Harald and Horic followed close, but Aun and Gnorre stayed aboard their own sea-home, binding each other's wounds.

In the excitement, Harald had scarcely noticed what manner of men they were fighting. Now it was obvious that they were coastwise Picts of Caledonia, men much like Wolf Waterhater. Harald turned to see that Wolf was still aboard the *Nameless*, cleaning the points of his mace and affecting not to notice what went on. Then Harald recalled that Wolf too was a Caledonian, and that these were his own people. He could understand why this terrible fighting-man did not wish to board the enemy.*

Now all was still. Thorkell, his wet hair swept back, and a shirt flung across his shoulders, was standing to face a group of Caledonians, who clustered about an old man

---

*History tells only of the most important happenings, the most forceful people. Sometimes it has to neglect the life of ordinary people so as to stress the victories of a king. So, always there is a part of any community that lags behind recorded history. There is always a part of any country that will not keep abreast of the beliefs of the times. There are people even today who believe that it is unlucky to sit thirteen at a table.

So, in many parts of what we now call Scotland, there were villages and even whole areas, in the eighth century, which had not become Christianized. This especially applied to the mountainous places, where communication was difficult.

And some of these folks, 'Picts' (or 'Painted ones,' as their Romanized name implies, because of their use of woad), still believed in the old gods, to whom sacrifices were made before the coming of Christ – such as Lugh, Mabon, and Belatucader.... Time moved slowly in those distant days.

Yet these people were not deficient in other respects. They were good fishers, good herdsmen, good craftsmen in iron and in the precious metals. It is not wise for us to belittle the intelligence, or the civilization, of any people simply because they do not hold the same religious beliefs as ourselves.

dressed in black robes, and wearing a round hat of cat-skin.

No one spoke for a while, each trying to break down the pride of the other. Then, at last, the old man whispered to a blood-stained warrior who stood beside him, and the man, wiping the drops of sweat from his tired eyes, translated to Thorkell. 'My master says that he intended no battle to you. He came to take what he thought was an abandoned ship. That is the law of the sea, in all Christendom.'

Thorkell said, 'We are not Christians, my friend. We are vikings. But say on. Perhaps you will tell us a story that will make us laugh.'

The man looked put out, but he turned again to his chief, the old man wearing the catskin cap, and listened to his instructions. Then he spoke again, 'My master says that he has nothing to offer you for the ransom of the crew and the ship, but that he will pray for the success of your enterprise farther north.'

Thorkell said, 'Thank your master for his prayers, and tell him that we pray to different gods. Tell him that we will be satisfied with his ship and with whatever cargo he carries.'

At this Ragnar smiled in his black beard, and Harald wondered what would come next. Then, to his great surprise, the old man in the catskin cap stepped slightly forward and said, without the aid of an interpreter, in good Norse, 'Young man, you are a knowing one. I will not try to deceive you further. We are not of the new religion, as you will know. I am a druid.'

He waited, expecting that the vikings might be impressed. But they were hard men who were not concerned with a man's religion, but only with their own gain, with fighting, with their own gods, with the nature of sea and herring-shoal. Thorkell said at last. 'We do not care what you call your gods. We fought you fairly for profit. Now we are entitled to your ship and to whatever she carries. We are also entitled to you – though Odin forbid that any of you scarecrows would interest us. If we were on our way back, well, we might take you with us as a midsummer sacrifice in the forests – but as slaves you would not be worth your carriage and victuals.'

Now the old man frowned, but Thorkell's smile and his glance at the sword he carried made him talk on.

'Young Berserk,' he said, 'we are not a rich folk, for we must often pay two dues, one to the Christian church and one to our own secret college. What we have here is dedicated to the sun god, Lugh. We came out to sink it in the waters for him, where he sets. To touch it would bring disaster upon yourselves and on us.'

Ragnar said, 'We will fend for ourselves. Show us the treasure.'

The vikings laughed, until they felt their longship jolt against the captured vessel, and sensed the deck-boards shuddering beneath them. Then they looked back in surprise. Wolf Waterhater was standing at the side of the *Nameless*, a long knife in his hand, the knife that had severed the grappling-ropes. His face was stern, so that even Thorkell knew that it would be of no avail to command him.

'What must we do, Wolf?' he said, seeing the widening space of sea between the ships.

Wolf Waterhater shrugged his shoulders and said, 'I

say, leave the Pictish ship, Thorkell, and let them sink their treasure where they will. That is what I say.'

Thorkell turned to the old man and said, 'Go your ways, father. My men and I will go back to our ship. May your old god help you in your need.'

The man in the black robes and the catskin cap smiled slowly and said, 'It is a pity that you do not give us back the man who cut the ropes. He is a Pict. I can see it in his face.'

Ragnar said bitterly, 'You can have him. He is a nuisance to our venture.'

Thorkell looked stern. He loved Wolf. Then from the *Nameless* Wolf's voice came back, 'No, black master, if you want me you must swim for me – as must all the others!'

With that he hoisted the sail again, and since he had a following wind, swept past the captured boat for a distance of three lengths. Then he threw down the staying-stone and waited.

The vikings laughed again and leapt overboard, to swim to the *Nameless*. Harald found himself in the salt water alongside Horic, who swam like a fish and ducked him many times before they boarded their own ship again.

When they were all aboard, Thorkell said, 'We have lost five men. Where are they?'

Aun and Gnorre got up from their seats and said, 'We did not wish to waste any time, Thorkell. We put them over, on the far side, while you were gossiping.'

Then they all laughed, all except Wolf, who seemed more interested in the strange signs that the old man in the black robes was making than in anything else.

'Come away, Wolf,' said Björn. 'He is not your master.'

Wolf shook his head sadly. 'One never knows, friend,' he said. 'Their arm is still a long one.'

Then Thorkell ordered the sail to be hoisted, and Harald noticed that the thin haze had become a clearly defined coastline.

Chapter **9** *The Visitor*

Darkness had settled on the rocky inlet where the *Nameless* lay. The vikings had lit a fire on the shore and clustered round it, wrapped in their sheepskins, eating pieces of salt pork, which they grilled on the ends of sticks.

Now, when the fight was long over, Harald found himself shivering from crown to toe with the delayed shock of the battle. He began to remember things he had seen at the time but had half-forgotten since, in the excitement of pulling in to shore. He remembered some of the horrors of the fight and Harald shuddered and turned away from the fire.

Behind him lay a dozen of the vikings, on heaps of sacking, all of them wounded, in leg or shoulder or chest. Kragge sat with Ivar, whose right arm hung limply from a great sword gash. Ivar was gripping his underlip with his teeth, trying not to show that he was in pain. Kragge was telling him some long story, meant to take his mind off his wound. But Ivar was not listening, Harald could see that.

Hasting had taken an axe blow across the thigh, and lay asleep near Björn, who washed the wide wound in fresh spring water to keep the inflammation away. As Harald came up, Björn smiled a little sadly and whispered, 'Hasting will not fight again, lad. The best he can hope for is a thatched hut and a herd of cows. He will go on a crutch for the rest of his days.'

Harald said, 'He would rather die, I think, Björn.'

Björn said, 'He may yet do that, Harald, for these are cold nights to be sleeping out in.'

Harald tried to make signs then that Hasting was awake, so that Björn should not say anything more. But Hasting had heard what was said. He made no reply, but only turned himself over and hid his face in the sacking.

Aun, Gnorre and Horic sat together, unscathed. They ate warm oat-cakes and drank corn-wine, which they had heated in their cups at the fire. They offered some to Harald, but he refused it, not liking its sour taste. He sat down beside them and said, 'We did not come out of that very well, did we?'

Aun said, 'It was a foolish venture, for we gained nothing and though we slew the greater part of their crew, we have lost some good men. Five I threw overboard my-

self, with Gnorre's aid, and here are two more who may not last the night out.' He nodded back to where Hasting and Ivar lay.

Gnorre said, 'Yet a start had to be made. A crew is not a crew until it has fought together, whatever the gain. That is the price one pays.'

Horic sat smiling, twisting his length of twine, saying nothing. Harald had the feeling that the Laplander did not care for battles, though he fought fiercely while in them.

'Now there will be nothing but rowing for us all,' said Aun. 'We have lost the relief-men, and unless we pick up two others when this night is over, you may still live to see Thorkell and Ragnar at the oars.'

Harald turned to look towards the leaders at this. They sat apart from the vikings, talking heatedly. Thorkell was waving his right hand about, and thumping it into the palm of his other, as though to emphasize the points he was making. Ragnar was shaking his head gravely. Harald wanted to creep nearer to them, to find out what they were saying, when there was a sudden blast on the horn from the viking who was acting as scout on the hill-top above. All men who could left the fire, for its glow would make them an easy target to anyone above who could use a bow. They ran into the shadows, drawing knives and swords, or unhooking the axes from their girdles.

There was a silence; then at last the sound of one man coming down the pebbled slope above them. Harald shivered as he heard the small stones falling on to the beach. He was not a coward, but he felt the spear he held shaking violently. He hoped that if there was to be an attack, he would not have to strike at anyone. He had not yet recovered from the shock of the earlier encounter; another on the same day would be too much.

Then a man came into the glow of the fires, and the flickering light glinted on the copper armbands and neck-ring which he wore. Upon his head he had a broad-brimmed iron helmet, which flung his face into shadow. A long parti-coloured cloak of red and green worsted hung from his shoulders, secured with a bronze brooch.

He was a small dark-haired man, though his shadow made him look bigger. He carried an iron-shod staff in his right hand, but no other weapon that could be seen.

Beside the fire he halted and looked round inquiringly, a smile on his dark face. Aun muttered, 'That is a brave man, to walk into our camp smiling and without a sword.'

'He claims a herald's privilege,' said Gnorre. 'He must come from the king of these parts, whoever he is.'

Now Thorkell stepped forward, his own sword sheathed, and said to the stranger, 'Do you come in peace?'

The dark man laughed and said, speaking Norse easily, 'I might ask the same question of you, viking, but I do not wish to insult you.'

Ragnar joined Thorkell. 'If I were to lay this blade once across your neck, you would join your fathers,' he said. 'How would you like that?'

The small dark man stared back at him and said, 'If I blew once upon this whistle, a hundred arrows would turn you into a hedgehog. How would you like that?'

Thorkell laughed and said, 'We are tired from a voyage and have lost some good men. If you wish to fight, let us wait till the morning, and when we have had a night's rest, we will come up the hill to you.'

The dark man said, 'I know of your fight this afternoon. It was my folk you killed. I am pleased to see that they gave a good account of themselves too. I am pleased, too, that you let my father sink his treasure where he wished. Had you taken it from him, we should have shot you through with arrows an hour ago when you were all round the fire. We are a lawless people in many ways, but we insist on serving our gods as we wish and without any hindrance.'

Ragnar said, 'You speak up bravely for a little man.' There was an insulting smile on his face as he spoke.

The other said, 'Better a small warrior than a tall coward.'

Ragnar said, 'There is light enough here for us to try each other's skill with any weapon you name.'

Thorkell was silent, for it was against the law for any man to prevent another from fighting, if he thought fit. Though they all saw that he was displeased with Ragnar. Even Hasting said, 'That Ragnar will be the end of us all, unless a check be put on him.'

Aun fingered his axe. 'I wish I might let Peacegiver talk a word to Ragnar,' he said.

'There may come a chance,' said Gnorre.

The small dark man by the fire glanced up the hill as though wondering whether he should blow his whistle. Then he shrugged his shoulders and said, 'If you will come to my steading as guests, so be it, and none shall harm you. If you still wish for death, so be it, and none shall hinder you from having it. I do not care. I only speak the words of my father who sent me to you.'

Thorkell held out both his hands and said, 'We come as guests, chieftain. I will speak for my crew. Is that good?'

The other said, 'That is good,' and took Thorkell's hands in his own.

It was at that moment that Aun saw Ragnar make a slight movement, as though to draw a knife. Such an act of treachery would bring death on them all, he knew. He sprang forward, dropping his axe on to the beach and flung both arms about Ragnar. In the shock of the impact, both men stumbled and fell. Even as they did so an arrow stuck quivering in the spot where Ragnar had been standing.

The vikings gasped. 'There are sharp eyes above us,' whispered Horic, smiling secretly. 'They see all.'

Thorkell still held the other's hands. They smiled at each other. 'Your friend is hot-tempered,' said the dark man. 'But then, it appears, so are my own watchers, so that makes all even.'

Now Aun let Ragnar rise again. For a while the two men glared at each other like wolves about to fight. 'I shall not forget you, Doorback,' said Ragnar darkly.

'I shall be ready for you, Raven,' said Aun. 'Come for me when you please.'

Then the vikings followed their leader up the hill, carrying their wounded, but leaving six men to keep a guard on the *Nameless* as she lay beached.

Chapter **10** *After the Feast*

After the feasting, Harald lay in the dark of the long pine hall, wide awake. He could not get off to sleep partly because of the excitements of the day, partly because of the groaning wounded who lay near the fire in the centre of the hall; but perhaps most of all because of the memories of the feast that had only just ended, memories which flooded in a great noisy tumult through his head.

Once again he heard the wild music of harp and flute that had filled the hall; he saw the dancers, skipping like elves above the crossed swords, their fierce faces lit with an ecstasy he had never observed on a man's face before. He saw in his mind's eye the long trestle table, with its torches set along it and the meat and drink scattered here and there in profusion. And at the head of the table, the old chief, Dubghal and his son, Feinn, with bright Thorkell between them, all of them laughing and singing as though they had known each other always. The boy recalled how, at a certain point in the feasting, Feinn had taken out his razor-keen hunting knife and had nicked Thorkell's wrist and his own and had placed them together so that their blood mingled.

Then the vikings and the Picts had roared with approval and had slapped each other so hard on the back that at least three fights started – and finished just as quickly when the old chieftain glared down the hall.

And he recalled poor Hasting and Ivar, propped up against the wall, their faces ashen pale, the food beside them untouched, their weak hands letting drop the wine horns that their comrades offered to them. Ivar had stared blindly towards the table, now without power of speech; Hasting had tried once or twice to speak to Aun, but could not make his voice heard above the general flurry of sound in the hall.

These things had impressed Harald deeply; but perhaps even more disturbing was his memory of Ragnar, seated down the table from his friend, brooding darkly and never saying a word to anyone, hacking savagely at the meat which was placed before him and drinking constantly of the strong heather-honey ale of which only the Picts held the secret. At first, they had all watched Ragnar anxiously, since they were afraid that he might start a quarrel out of jealousy. Yet as the evening wore on, and nothing untoward had happened, they had forgotten him.

Once Thorkell had looked round the table and had asked for Wolf, but no man had seen Wolf that night. Someone said that he had volunteered to stay with the *Nameless*, and that had satisfied Thorkell. The old chief, Dubghal had said wryly, 'That Wolf is one of our folk, I think. I should like to speak with him.'

The young chief had said quickly, 'He has lived with the Northmen almost all his life, father. You cannot call on him.'

Harald had wondered what this meant and Horic had said in a whisper, 'They of the old faith choose a red-haired one to lie on the stone at Midsummer. I think Wolf was wise to stay with the *Nameless*. It is every man's right to choose the manner of his own death!'*

Then, when the Picts had sung and told their stories, the old man Dubghal had asked if any of the vikings had a skill in entertaining, and Horic had been pushed forward to do his winter dance on the long table. This time he improved on his earlier performance, for he brought the creatures of air and forest into the very hall. Standing in the flickering torchlight, he had extended his long arm towards the rooftree, and everyone had not only heard, but seen the wild geese coming down from Iceland and flying south through the firesmoke, to disappear before they reached the far wall. Then a bear had walked in at one door and out of another. At last a wolf had howled outside the hall and Horic had made the motion of inviting it in; but by this time the Picts had had enough of the illusion and the old chief, afraid that one of them might hurt the Laplander in his excitement, had bidden the entertainment to stop. Later he had called Horic to him and had offered him much gold to stay with them, for he knew that the Laplander was of the same old faith which he himself followed. But Horic had shaken his head and had said that he only did these things for amusement's sake, and that if he were forced to do them, his power would leave him. So Dubghal had reluctantly let the little man take his place at the foot of the table once more.

And Harald recalled all these things as he lay in the darkened hall, the feast now ended. Here and there

---

*Horic was referring to the druidic sacrifices, performed on Midsummer Day, at dawntime, when a red-haired youth was chosen to represent the Sun-god. By dying on the sacrificial stone, this youth was thought to bring sunshine and hence growth to the crops. He died for the people.

through the gloom, dark figures moved, though whether they were vikings or Picts the boy did not know. And at times a strange whispering started up and seemed to pass through the hall before it faded and died. There was an air of general unrest about. But at last Harald fell into a light, troubled sleep, in which green-eyed wolves looked round the trunks of pine trees at him and called to him in Ragnar's voice. . . .

Then suddenly Harald was awake again. The fire had gone out completely now, but the hall was full of movement. Then there was the flash of flint on iron and a torch flamed out. Harald saw that the vikings were on their feet, their weapons drawn. There was a great shout in his ear. Aun yelled, 'Out steel, we are betrayed.' Then the hall was full of leaping shapes and swords rose and fell, vicious in the dim light.

Harald found himself between Aun and Gnorre. Horic was somewhere behind them, grunting as he struck out. A Pict, wearing feathers in his helmet, came at them. Harald saw the mad light in his eyes as the man thrust out with a long leaf-bladed sword. The weapon seemed to flash before the boy's very eyes, then the man screamed and tumbled forward with the impetus of his rush, almost knocking Harald's feet from under him. Aun bent and swung up his axe again. Gnorre said, 'Don't fall, lad, or it will be your end. Keep your feet and we may win to the door.'

They began a slow rhythmic movement across the hall. They passed Björn, who stood over the bodies of Hasting and Ivar. He was beset on every side, but spared a word as he swung his axe. 'Do not stay, Aun Doorback,' he said. 'If Odin wills it, I shall come down to the ship again. If not, then he means me to travel with these two vikings home.'

Harald saw that Hasting and Ivar had not survived their wounds, gained earlier in the sea-fight. Then he saw Thorkell at the far end of the hall, surrounded by their dark-skinned enemies. Feinn, with whom he had taken the blood-oath that night, pressed close at him, taunting him. 'So this is what men mean when they say: "Trust a viper before a viking!" I had not thought you would so soon forget your friend's promise.'

Thorkell swept his long blade about the circle that tried to close on him. 'It is you, Feinn, who are the breaker of vows. I have done nothing worse than trying to get a night's sleep since I last saw you.'

Feinn and his followers laughed in derision, and lunged in at the golden-haired leader.

Gnorre looked round and said, 'I do not see Ragnar, or any of those who follow him rather than Thorkell. Come, Aun, we must spare a blow for Thorkell before we go!'

The four of them pressed forward to where their leader fought. He was a fine sight, even though outnumbered. His hair was disarranged and his shirt of mail pulled on carelessly. Even the strappings of his hide breeches dangled behind him as he shuffled now in this direction, now in that, to meet and slash at a foeman. Yet, for all that, he looked a hero, even the son of Thor himself, thought Harald.

Aun yelled, 'Up Thorkell! Up the *Nameless*!' Gnorre joined him in the cry, but Horic and Harald were silent. Yet all pushed on, and now, with the men beside him, even Harald felt a strange desire for battle. It seemed to him that now they were fighting with good cause, and not merely to win treasure. They were fighting a

treacherous enemy, for their very lives, and to save their leader, to whom they had pledged themselves.

They took the Picts by surprise. Some of them turned at Aun's first shout and put up sword or small buckler as defence. But two at least of them were too late. Peace-giver rose and fell, rose and fell. Horic's rough sword thrust to left and to right. Then a bundled dark shape launched itself at Harald. He heard Gnorre's shout of warning, but it came too late. The man was on him, stabbing furiously with a short dagger. Harald felt the blade sear his shoulder, and then, in a great anger, he shortened his spear, and using it like a sword, struck with all his force at the man who attacked him. He felt the jar of the blow along his arm and then the man seemed to run on past him, sideways, dragging the spear from his grasp.

Gnorre said, 'Your first blood! Hail viking! Thorkell shall give you another weapon now.'

Harald's heart swelled, for he saw Thorkell's eyes glance at him and a grim smile come across his leader's face. Thorkell had seen him fight his first battle. Then a great wave of nausea swept over the boy, and he wished that the Pict had never run at him.

The next thing he knew, he was standing next to Thorkell, and they were all pushing their terrible way to the open door, through which Harald saw the stars shining out of a deep blue-black sky.

Behind them, still clustered in the hall, were their enemy. Feinn was leaning against the wall, his hand over his chest, the dark blood ebbing between his white fingers, a vicious grin on his swarthy face.

Harald heard him gasp, 'Thorkell Traitor, though you leave me so, my gods will follow you. Their arm is long.'

Thorkell's face twisted in a smile of sadness. It was as though he wished to go to Feinn. Then with a shrug he remembered where he was and they turned to go through the door into the night.

Yet, even as they turned, a dark shape lying in the doorway moved. A man raised himself on his elbow and flung the short axe he had clenched in his hand. The blow was meant for Thorkell, but Gnorre saw the axe as it flew through the air and stepped towards it, keeping it from the leader. Harald heard the haft thud on Gnorre's temples, and stepped across to catch him as he fell. Aun gave a great roar of anger and struck down towards the floor. The man lay still.

Gnorre was unconscious and the blood flowed down his face. Aun took him on to his broad back and carried him. Horic and Thorkell paused for a moment in the doorway. They called to Björn, but he would not come. He still stood over the bodies of his comrades, singing quietly to himself, a terrible rhythm of death, like the song that oarsmen sing when they battle against a contrary tide.

'Up – ay – aa ! Up – ay – aa !'

His sword struck again and again. His eyes were glazed. He did not know where he was, it seemed.

Thorkell whispered, 'Odin holds out his hands for Björn. He will never come away now.'

Then he called out softly, 'Farewell, viking. We must go down to the ship your hands built. May they build even better ships where you are going.'

Harald felt the hot tears running down his cheeks. He saw that Thorkell was crying too. As they turned, Björn snatched up a pine torch and was swinging it round him as he shambled towards the ring of men who waited, like hungry wolves, for his great strength to fail.

When they were half-way down the hill that gave on to the beach, they looked back at the sudden glow in the sky behind them.

'Björn has made himself a funeral pyre,' said Aun. 'Now if Feinn lives, he must build himself another hall !'

Then they saw the *Nameless*. She was already afloat and ready to move away. Thorkell shouted, and down below them Ragnar answered, 'Hurry, Thorkell,' he said. 'We had given you up for lost. The tide pulls us away. Hurry !'

They struggled over the rough shingle and on into the water, breast-high before they reached the longship. Rough hands dragged them aboard. Harald saw Gnorre's eyes flicker, and he heard him whisper something to Aun, who bent over him like a mother over her child.

Horic whispered, 'Gnorre's wound is not deep, lad. Sleep happily.'

Then Harald fell his length on the hard wet boards, exhausted in body and in mind. He did not hear the gulls crying or the wind slapping against the great mainsail. He did not hear Thorkell's harsh words to Ragnar, or Ragnar's ironical laughter. Nor did he hear Ragnar say, 'You are a fool, Thorkell. I and my band raided their treasure house while you slept. We have brought enough away to make us all rich men. And that is the thanks I get !'

Thorkell said, 'You traitorous dolt ! I had taken a blood-oath with Feinn.'

Ragnar pulled at his black beard and said, 'The oath bound you, not me, my friend !'

Harald did not see Thorkell strike the Dane full across the face then, for all men to watch. The boy was deep in sleep.

Chapter **II** *Harald's Dream*

The *Nameless* rode wearily in the northern sea. It was now the best part of a week since she had put out from the rocky inlet under Feinn's steading. It was such a week as made Harald think lovingly of the days when he lived ashore in Gudröd's hall, with solid ground beneath his feet, a good meal three times a day and a warm bed to go to at night, out of the winds. The northern sea held no such comforts. Often the vikings were wet and hungry, and often they must watch or row all night so that they might sleep in the sunshine on deck the next day. Harald thought many times of his father, almost tearfully now, wondering if his leg had mended well. . . .

During the week since the fight in the hall, the *Nameless* had put into shore twice, when Thorkell had sighted smoke rising above a village. They had been lucky enough to attack without warning and had carried away enough provisions to keep them fed, but without any luxuries. The first village had been an easy one to surprise, since most of the men were away on a hunting trip into the mountains. They had stormed the low stockade and had carried off meal and meat. Kragge had fired a hut or two before anyone could stop him. In this affray Wolf had stolen a little pig, but a small black-haired girl ran after him towards the longship, crying so bitterly that he had stopped and given it back. He gave the child a bracelet from his arm, after which she wanted to come with him on to the *Nameless*. But Thorkell made him take the child back, almost to the gates of the village. As he waved good-bye to her, an enthusiastic shepherd put an arrow through Wolf's ear, which caused him great discomfort and made his comrades laugh, to see him jumping with rage, shaking his fist at the marksman, and waving to the little girl – all at the same time.

The second foraging expedition was not so fortunate, generally. It was a much larger settlement, some of its houses being made of stone. The vikings got into it easily enough, for it was night-time and the place was poorly guarded. But once inside, they found it more difficult to make their escape. Both women and men attacked the vikings with whatever weapons lay at hand. One buxom woman laid open Kragge's head with an iron ladle. Three others caught Rolf and flung him into a deep midden pit, almost dislocating his steering arm. It was only with great difficulty that Aun and Gnorre pulled the steersman up again, after which all men walked at some distance from him.

While this foray went on, men from a neighbouring settlement made a detour and got down to the *Nameless* in the shallow bay. They were still striking at the ship's sides with heavy wood-axes when Thorkell's band returned. Luckily Björn had built a ship to last and they had done little damage when the vikings trapped them, between the cliff and the sea. At first Thorkell would have struck off their heads, on the sand, for his anger was so great that a plank of the *Nameless* should have been touched by an enemy. Then he listened to Ragnar's counsel, and took the protesting men aboard to act as oarsmen, and later to be sold as slaves. They all felt that they deserved this fate, since they had interfered in a quarrel that did not concern them and had tried to damage a fine ship which had done them no harm.

The captured half-dozen were young red-faced foresters, well used to hard work. They were chained at the ankles, but their arms were left free, so that they might row without hindrance.

At first they were wrathful and silent. They even dared to sneer in Thorkell's face when he spoke to them, telling them that if they behaved themselves he would try to find a good master to sell them to. But their bravado soon left them as the *Nameless* pulled out farther and farther into the northern sea. Then first one, then another broke down and wept. They began to implore Thorkell to set them ashore again and promised that they would pay a handsome price for their freedom. This made the vikings laugh, for they knew that the men were lying, and had no more money than would buy a truss of hay for a horse. So it was that the twelve men of the *Nameless* who had been lost in the earlier fighting were replaced by the six Pictish slaves. It was a poor exchange, but better than none, for by now the ship had need of every hand she could find.

The quarrel between Ragnar and Thorkell had healed itself, up to a point, and now even Thorkell liked to lift the deckboards and gaze down on the great bundles of gold torques and gorgets and drinking-cups that they had amassed in that treacherous raid.

So, one way and another, the voyage went fairly well until a storm blew up late one afternoon and carried them eastwards, far from any land. One man of the *Nameless* was swept away when a great wave struck the ship on the beam. He was a viking named Smörke, who had lost three brothers in the northern sea already. He had often said that this voyage would be his last, but all had laughed at him. As he was swept overboard, Gnorre swore that he heard the man yell out, 'There, I told you so!'

They all ran to the side, but there was nothing to be done. Smörke was borne away in a swirl of water, and the last men saw of him were the bull's horns of his helmet.

'That will confuse Odin,' said Horic. 'He will think that Smörke died in battle. A man should have the sense to take off his helmet if he is going to die in the sea.'

But for all that, the vikings were sorry to lose a good sailor. Yet the storm was so violent that they did not mourn for long. Their attention was needed for other things.

Harald suddenly felt older, much older. Now the sea was an enemy, he thought, a ravenous salt beast that for ever gnawed at the timbers of a boat, and no friend. The boy smiled bitterly as he recalled his joy on setting out over the fjord, so long ago it seemed now. He remembered the smooth glassy sea, so harmless and so mirror-like, a deep blue-bronze, with the rich amber sun shining across it.

Harald stood upright, clutching the swinging gunwales, the bitter salt spray smashing hard at his face and over his drenched body. He remembered Gryffi with the spear in him, Björn swinging the torch in the great hall, the faces of Ivar and Hasting as they sat dumbly against the wall, the man he had killed. . . .

He did not feel the spray then. He was lost in a dream, his wet golden hair stuck across his wind-reddened face; his cloak heavy with sea-water, yet flung out in fitful gusts behind him as the gale tore at it, making its edges ragged. Harald's pale-blue eyes stared blindly through the thick spume. He did not see it, did not feel the storm, even for a moment. Now he was back in memory on the fjord, with the amber sun staring at him from the west, casting a broad track towards him, magnificent and grim as blood. And over this ghastly sea of his memory, a deep and echoing voice seemed to say, 'Come, young viking. Come, come, come, come. Walk on the Whale's Way, pace the Path of the Dolphin towards me. Come to the sun, warrior-lad, come, come, come. . . .'

He began to sway on his feet, and it was then that Aun caught him and carried him into shelter under one of the platforms. 'The lad is suffering from a fever,' he said to Thorkell. 'He has seen too much and suffered too much since we started out.'

'Yet he shapes well,' said Thorkell. 'He will make a good viking yet.'

Aun said, 'He won't unless we treat that wound in his shoulder. The young fool has said nothing to anyone about it, and now it is inflamed and swollen. If you won't care for the lad, as you ought, since his father is maimed for you, then let me take him over. I am prepared to do my duty if you are not.'

At first Thorkell was angry that Aun Doorback should speak like that to him. Then he made himself smile as he said, 'I am sorry, Aun Doorback. I have had little experience at being a father to anyone. But I shall improve with time. Have patience with me, and in the meantime, let us both be father to the lad.'

So it was that Harald found himself a second father, in the middle of the northern sea in a storm. He almost found death too, that night, for the ship's mast snapped and crashed through the roof where he lay, missing him by the breadth of a child's hand. Yet such was the lad's fever that he knew nothing of these things for many days, until he was told.

Chapter **12** *A Ship and a Sword*

In the days that followed, the vikings were beset by sore trials. Now though the storm wore itself out, they had to row from dawn to dusk to make headway. Their hands were raw and their backs breaking. One of the slaves fell into a stupor and at last lay still. Thorkell had him put overboard for there was no one to tend him. Then the fresh water ran out and now men dared not row for thirst. They tried drinking corn-wine instead, but that left them stupefied and witless and they lolled about the decks, disinterested in life. Nothing that Thorkell or Ragnar could do would rouse them.

It was while they were in this condition that a cargo-vessel passed them, at a distance of not much more than a hundred feet. It was a high round-bellied tub, carrying two sails, a Frankish trader, a privateer, laden with amber and bear-pelts and reindeer hides; a ship of the south, anxious to spoil the icy north, crewed with hard men who felt themselves to be man for man as good as any viking of the fjords. This ship had sailed in upon a quiet village, too busy with its own affairs to think of guards, and had come away laden to the gunwales with enough barbaric finery to keep the Frankish Court in high glee for long enough. Thorkell had quickly judged it to be a Frankish ship, and wished that they could have boarded it. But the merchants on board the vessel could see the sorry plight of the vikings, as they rolled on the decks of their mastless ship, and they came to the side of their boat and looked down on them, jeering. When Ragnar shouted back at them, they challenged him to come aboard and fight their champion on the foredeck. Such was Ragnar's rage that he would have gone, not seeing that it was a trick. But Thorkell held him back, and the Franks passed on unharmed and laughing.

'One day you will laugh on the other side of your face,' yelled Ragnar, who hated to be bested.

'Good riddance!' shouted the Franks, and Black Ragnar beat his forehead on the gunwales with rage.

The following morning, shortly after dawn, another viking longship rode confidently up alongside them and flung grappling irons over the side of the *Nameless*. Her seamen could see well enough the plight of Thorkell's ship and looked for an easy prize, but when their leader saw who was captain of the *Nameless* he climbed aboard and flung his arms round Thorkell and kissed him on the cheeks. It turned out to be his cousin, Knud, whom he had not seen for three years. Knud gave the vikings two kegs of water and a sack of meal. He told them that if they steered due west they would strike an easy coast where the forests came down to the sea. There they might make another mast from some tall tree.

In return, Thorkell told Knud that a big Frankish trader had passed them but a few hours before. Knud slapped him on the back and said, 'Tit for tat! If I take anything worth having, I will keep a share for you!'

Then his longship, which he called *Hungry Hawk*, set course and bore down after the ship which had so insulted

Ragnar. 'Strike off the captain's head for me,' yelled Ragnar. Knud laughed back. He was more interested in plunder than in killing.

During the days that followed Harald slowly recovered from the effects of his exhaustion and of the poisoned shoulder which had laid him low. Aun and Gnorre took it in turns to sit with him and to put cold water pads on his arm and chest to keep down the fever. Horic and Rolf came when they could and told him tales when he was able to understand them again.

Horic had a lovely yarn about two brothers who went hunting bear in the great forest of Lapland. Their names were Festi and Vlasta, and they were great hunters but a little simple in all other respects. One night as they sat by their fire, Festi saw a big bear looking at them. He told his brother to make ready the pot and took his bear-knife and went after the animal. The bear ran away, but Festi soon caught up with it and, after a short struggle, was able to kill it. Then he thought that he would play a joke on his brother, so he skinned the bear and got into the skin, intending to frighten him. He made his way silently back through the woods until he came to a rock, near the fire where he had left his brother and, after making a great growling, leapt out into the firelight. But instead of his brother, a great bear sat by the fire, just finishing off the last of Vlasta. The real bear and the imitation bear stared at each other for a while, then each gave a yell and ran away, the bear back into the forest, and Festi to his village. But when the villagers saw Festi coming, they thought that he was the great bear that had terrified them for so long. Three strong men ran to meet him, and put three arrows into him as he ran towards them, because he was so wrapped about with bear-skin that they did not recognize his shouts for help.

Most of Horic's stories were about bears. And they usually ended with someone getting eaten. He would roar with laughter when he came to that part and would rock backwards and forwards until he made Harald feel quite giddy. Then Rolf would come in and tell Horic not to be a barbarian. He would push him out and try to teach Harald the art of navigation. Rolf was a very kind person in spite of his forbidding appearance, and Harald came to like him as much as any of the vikings.

One day Thorkell came into the hut below the platform. He smiled down at Harald wearily. The boy saw that the warrior's hands were calloused and raw, as though from much rowing. He moved with a bent back, stiffly. His fine golden hair was tangled and matted now, and was tied in a rough knot. His blue eyes were red-rimmed and tired.

'It has been a hard row, viking,' he said to Harald. 'You must hasten and get well, then you can give us a hand.'

When the tears of weakness gathered in the boy's eyes, Thorkell bit his lips and looked sheepishly down at the floor.

'I was teasing, lad,' he said. 'There will be time enough another day, mayhap. Look, Aun tells me it is time to bring you these gifts.'

He put two packages on to Harald's lap, one as small as his hand, the other as long as his arm, both wrapped in oiled cloth. Harald tried to unwrap the small one, but his sick fingers only fumbled at the knot which held the package together. Thorkell took the gift and slashed the string

with his knife. Then carefully he unwound the cloth. A perfectly carved model of a viking longship lay in his hand, gleaming white, fragile and beautiful. Harald gave a gasp of excitement. His hands lay on the sheepskin coverlet. Thorkell put the ship on the boy's lap, where he could touch it.

'Björn made it,' said Thorkell. 'It is of ivory that someone brought from Byzantium long ago. Björn carved it when he made his first voyage, when they were becalmed in the White Sea. He told me that he wanted to give it to you after your first battle. He is not here to give it. It is yours, Harald Sigurdson.'

Harald remembered poor Björn, fighting alone in the long hall, a torch in his hand. The tears filled his eyes again.

Thorkell said, 'Do not weep for Björn. That is the death he wanted. He is a lucky man. Not all of us will die so well.'

He unwrapped the long package. Harald watched him and saw, slowly revealed, a sword. At the sight of it he felt exhausted again with wonderment and could only sigh. The polished hilt was of ebony, inlaid with rings of silver; the pommel was a globe of rock-crystal, carved into the shape of an acorn; the guard was a curved cross-piece of bronze, chiselled to form ivy tendrils curling round a bough; the blade was long and leaf-shaped, with thin runnels going its length, from hilt to point. It shone blue-black in the dim light of the cabin. He did not dare to touch it.

Thorkell smiled happily. 'Take this,' he said. 'It was made for me when I was but a little older than you are now. It was my warrior-gift after I had been lucky in my first foray. Now I give it to you, and may it bring such luck to you as it has done to me.'

When he had said that, he laid the sword across the boy's knees and went from the cabin, turning back only once, to smile down at Harald. The boy gazed stupidly at the two precious gifts and wished that his father were there to see them. Then he fell into a contented sleep, and dreamed that he was running down the path back to Gudröd's hall with the gifts in his hand to show his father. And when the door opened at his shouts, he saw that not only his father but his mother also stood on the threshold, waiting to welcome him. And Harald wept in his sleep, for his mother had died when he was very small, and he could not recall her face.

It was while he was weeping thus, in his sleep, that Aun came in and shook him gently and woke him.

'Good fortune!' he said. 'We have run upon a fleet of Orkney fishermen, eight smacks in all. They will tow us back with them.'

Harald said, 'Are they our own people?'

Aun answered, 'Yes, all northmen, though they sailed out to Orkney a generation ago. We are in luck's way, Harald. Now you will get well again, and we shall have no more rowing for a while at least!'

As he finished, a strange man wearing a woollen cap over his grey hair looked into the cabin. 'Is this the young warrior?' he said, and Aun nodded. The man came forward and gently examined his shoulder. 'My wife, Asa, will know what to do with that,' he said. 'She is a great woman for herbs.'

'That is Olaf,' said Aun. 'He is a fisherman and a farmer, and has a family of his own; a prosperous man, who will look after us now.'

And truly the vikings of the *Nameless* needed someone to look after them, for the breaking of their mast came near to costing them their lives. No man had tasted water for two days, and they were too weak to battle any longer against the sea which seemed determined to keep them from the shore. Yet, even though they suffered agonies of thirst, they had agreed to let the sick boy have what water there was. Harald never knew this. No viking would tell him a thing like that.

Chapter 13 *Olaf's Steading*

Olaf's hall was a comfortable place, built solidly of wood and set in the shelter of a large rocky hill. A great fire of driftwood always burned, and Asa saw that the rushes on the floor were changed regularly, although her sons grumbled at having to do this. There was enough work cleaning out the byre and gutting the fish, they said. But they always obeyed their mother.

Asa was a plump woman with a red, smiling face. Her fair hair was bound in a scarf of blue linen. Her sleeves were always rolled back over her strong arms, for there was ever a job to do, either milking or baking or washing, and she had no daughters to help her – only three huge sons, lazy louts, she called them, though she loved them dearly.

Asa's great sons were all red-headed, as their father had been before he became grey. They were Sven, Rollo and Ottar. Each day they could, they went down to help in the task of getting the *Nameless* ready for her next voyage.

The battered longship lay, a hawk among gulls, in the midst of the fishing-smacks, in the little grey-stone harbour under the shadow of Olaf's hill. Seabirds screamed over her as the men worked hard, stepping the new mast, renewing the tackle and recaulking the seams. Thorkell was hard at work every day, whatever the weather. He gave himself no rest. His once-beautiful eyes were now always red-rimmed and bloodshot. The winds were cruel to the eyes.

Under Asa's care, Harald grew well again, though at first she had almost despaired of him. Once she came to his bedside when he lay in a troubled sleep, crying out to his father, telling him of the man he had killed. Asa saw the boy's pale hands and his sunken face. She saw the sword and the ivory longship that he always had at the side of his bed, and for a moment she had an impulse to destroy them in her anger.

'A fine lot of warriors you are, to bring a lad to this, with your swords and silly boats,' she said to Aun, who only scratched his head and looked away. 'Butchers, I call you! I pray that Odin never puts such tomfoolery into my lads' heads!'

But her prayer was made a little too late. Asa's three huge sons grew to love the *Nameless* as they worked on her in the harbour, and one day when they were shown the treasure that was placed for safety in their father's strong-room, their eyes glistened with envy. That night they told their father that they wished to sail with the *Nameless* when she left again. Olaf shrugged his shoulders. He did not tell them that it would be hard for him to make a living without them, farming and fishing. He only said, 'You are of age. You will do as you please.'

That night he said to his wife, 'We must pull in our belts a little when the boys have gone.'

Asa flew into a great rage, but she saw that it was no use arguing. Olaf had left his people in Norway, and she hers. Their sons were only doing the same. 'Very well,' she said at last, when her eyes were dry, 'then I shall keep Harald to make up for them. He shall be our son.'

Olaf smiled sadly and patted her gently on the shoulder. 'He is worse than our lads,' he said. 'He is already a viking. They are only fisherfolk, though they have big arms and bigger ideas !'

And Asa knew that he was right. The next day she asked Harald if he would stay, but he shook his head and said, 'I have a father already, Asa, and I promised him to make the voyage. He lies sick and I must go back to him one day. Besides, I am pledged to Thorkell and must follow him until he sets me free.'

Not all men were so loyal to the young leader, however. While the vikings were resting on the island, Kragge went round to many of them, spreading tales of Thorkell's lack of leadership. Many now began to look to Ragnar, who had after all got them the treasure they carried. Indeed, before a month was out, only a handful still thought of Thorkell as their true shipmaster. These included Rolf, Aun, Gnorre, Horic and, of course, Wolf. Harald did not know of this treachery, but even if he had, Thorkell's place in his affection was too high for him to be replaced by any living man but Harald's own father.

At last the *Nameless* was ready again, and looking as bright and fresh as when she had been launched. Provisions were laid aboard, and there was some feasting in Olaf's great hall, though it had an air of sadness about it now. Olaf's sons were there, and three of their cousins, big men like themselves, who wished to leave the island and sail away on their adventures.

They were all waiting to take the oath, but Thorkell was still down at the harbour, with the longship. At last he came up the path to the hall. All men heard his slow, shuffling step. They watched him stand by the doorway for a while, fingering the rough wood of the doorposts. When he looked up, his half-closed eyes seemed to look beyond them. Olaf said, 'Drink a cup of wine in celebration of your sailing, Thorkell.' And he stepped forward and handed a cup to the young shipmaster. But Thorkell put out his hand to the side of the cup and grasped the empty air. Men drew in their breath. Olaf led Thorkell towards a chair, but he could not see it and fell down beside it. Gnorre whispered, 'He is blind. Great Thor, we have a blind captain!' Then all men except his friends shrank from Thorkell. They helped him to his feet and led him weeping to his bed.

That night, Olaf's sons and their cousins took the oath to Ragnar, and the others, who sided with Ragnar, took the oath again, now no longer Thorkell's men.

When Wolf went to comfort Thorkell, the young leader struck out at him, but Wolf only smiled and put his arms about him.

'I will be your eyes, Thorkell Fairhair,' he said, 'You have lost nothing.'

'I will be your right arm, Thorkell Fairhair,' said Aun. 'You have gained something.'

'I will be your spell-master, Thorkell Fairhair,' said Horic, crying a little as he said it. 'You will gain everything.'

'Where is Harald,' said Thorkell, pushing them away. 'Where is my young viking?'

Harald stepped forward and stood by Thorkell. The leader put his hand on the boy's shoulder and said, 'Are you with me, lad?'

Harald said, 'I would try to kill anyone who asked me that but you, Master.'

Thorkell smiled then and said, 'So be it. Now I know that I have lost little.' And with that he fell into an exhausted slumber while his friends watched over him.

Asa turned Thorkell's eyelids up as he slept. She said to Aun, 'I have seen such blindness before among those who come here. It is the bitter wind which scours our island and blows dust into the eyes.'

Aun said, 'Will he see again?'

Asa said, 'Only Odin can say that. I have known such eyes to see again. He should stay here indoors and not go on to the sea.'

Aun answered, 'He would rather be blind than leave the sea.'

Asa said, 'He is a fool then, like you, and like my own sons. One would think their mothers were seals. Look, I will give you herbs with which you must make a poultice, then bandage them to his eyes. He must be kept quiet, in the dark and away from the wind. Then perhaps Odin might take pity on him and let him see. Who knows? We can only do our best.'

Aun turned to Harald and said, 'Thorkell is a difficult man to treat. He will knock my teeth out if I try to make him sit still. You are the one to do it, boy. He will listen to you.'

The next day a great crowd of islanders gathered above the stone harbour, and a pathway was cleared for the longship between the clustered fishing-boats. The vikings went aboard, led by Ragnar, who took Kragge as his second-in-command. Wolf and Thorkell came last. Harald led

Thorkell by the hand and many women wept as they watched this. As Thorkell went up the plank, he stumbled and almost fell into the water. One of Olaf's sons said, 'Thank goodness we have a leader who can see.'

Ragnar heard these words and strode down the long-ship to where the man sat. He said in a loud voice for all to hear, 'Though the vikings have elected me their leader, Thorkell is still my blood-brother, young sniffling. Were we in open sea, I would have you whipped for what you have said. But since we have not started, then get up and go back to your cow-byre where you belong.'

The young man's face flushed with embarrassment. He said, 'I am sorry, Ragnar. I will beg Thorkell's pardon.'

He went to Thorkell and knelt before him but Thorkell pushed him aside and paid no heed to him. Ragnar felt that the young man had been punished enough and sent him back to his seat.

Olaf, at the dockside, was furious with his son and wanted to go aboard and thrash him. But Asa said grimly, 'Leave him be, husband. Between the two of them, that Ragnar and that Thorkell will bring the young lout to his senses!'

When the *Nameless* sailed, Thorkell sat in the darkness of the rear cabin, with Harald by his side. Now he obeyed the boy for he trusted him in a way that he trusted no other man on board, not even faithful Wolf, who would have leapt overboard at the merest whisper from his master.

While they were still rowing and before their sail had caught a good wind, Ragnar stood on the forward plat-form and spoke to all the vikings. He said, 'Sea-warriors, we sail southwards now for Ireland where there is great treasure in the holy places. The Christ-men lay up great stores of gold. It does no good lying there in the dark. We northmen can use it to good advantage. Let it be ours to take back to the fjord. How say you?' And they all roared and cheered these words, save only Thorkell's friends.

In the darkness, Thorkell said, 'These same Christ-men can bear pain, they tell me. Is it so?'

Gnorre said, 'They are men, like anyone else. Any man will bear pain if he has to.'

Wolf said, 'I think they are more than ordinary men. I have heard that their holy men go out of their way to find pain, so that they may master it.'

'I have heard that, too,' said Aun. 'Their leader did just that, in the time of the Romans. He seemed to seek death, so at last the Romans gave it to him, when they nailed him on to a cross.'

'I like the sound of these Christ-men,' said Thorkell. 'They would make good vikings.'

'Many of them were vikings, long ago,' said Wolf. 'They went to Britain in their own sort of longship when the Romans were there.'

'I beg your pardon,' said Gnorre, 'but the Romans had gone.'

'I tell you the Romans were there,' said Wolf.

'It all depends on what you mean by Romans,' said Thorkell, his mind taken off his pain for a while. 'So they were vikings, were they?'

'In a way, ' said Wolf, 'though they went to stay, not to plunder like us and then to go back home.'

Aun scratched his head. 'What difference does it make where you live?' he said. 'There is only eating and drinking and sleeping, call it home, call it what you will.'

Thorkell, who loved an argument, as did most north-men, especially if it were on a point of life or death, said, 'Some ways of living are better than others. A man's life is better than a pig's, for instance. Do you deny that?'

Aun said, 'No, but a god's life is better than a man's.'

'Yes,' said Gnorre, 'the gods feast and fight all the time and never have to row longships through contrary tides.'

Thorkell said, 'How do you know what the gods do? Have you ever seen them? Do you know anyone who has seen them?'

Gnorre said, 'No, but every man *knows* that the gods do this or that. It is in the stories.'

Horic said, 'In my stories bears can talk, but have you ever heard bears talk?'

Aun said, 'Be quiet, Horic, you are simple and do not understand arguments about these things.'

Thorkell said, 'Horic is right though. We know nothing for sure. We do not even know whether we shall eat our dinner today. I did not know I would be blind, but I am blind.'

Aun said, 'Do you deny that we shall go to Odin when we die, then?'

Thorkell said, 'I cannot answer that, but I will tell you a story. Two vikings sat in a longship, chained to a log, for they had been taken prisoners in a sea-fight. They had such an argument as we are having now. Then one of them said, "Look, the headsman is coming with his axe. We shall soon know the answer, friend." The other one said, "I am first so I shall know first." His friend said, "That is a pity, for you will not be able to tell me. Let me go first." But the other said, "No, it is my turn. But look, I will take this cloak pin, and if I know anything after my head is off, I will stick the pin into the log I am sitting on. Then you will know." And that was what they agreed to do.'

'What happened?' said Harald, who had been listening excitedly, though not daring to speak before.

Thorkell grinned. 'When the axe fell, the pin dropped out of the viking's fingers.'

'So nobody knew,' said Gnorre.

'Oh yes they did,' said Wolf. 'It is obvious, even to a fool like you, that there was nothing after death.'

'No,' shouted Aun, 'only obvious that there was no control of one's fingers after death, and any fool should know that, even you, redhead!'

By which time Thorkell was in a fine good humour, in spite of the glowing pain that never lessened, and the *Nameless* was well out in the open sea and setting a course south-westwards.

Chapter **15** *Leire's Dun*

Leire's Dun was built on a promontory, backed by a gaunt purple mountain. Though to say built is not an accurate description; it had been added to as occasion demanded, its houses of widely differing types flung together helter-skelter in haste. At first there had been only a rough stone hut, to which Leire had come from Ireland, foraging. He had killed the shepherd who built the hut and had lived there himself, his small boat having been wrecked on the treacherous rocks that lined the narrow channel below the neck of land. Soon he was joined by others, each of whom had made a house for himself, of wood or wattle or rough stone mortared with mud. That was many years ago, though Leire's descendants still ruled as chieftains in the place. Now there was a street and a square of sorts in Leire's Dun, and in the square a strong-room, sometimes used for storing wood or even fish, sometimes for keeping prisoners for whom a ransom was expected. For Leire's Dun was nothing more nor less than a pirate stronghold. The custom of the place was to lure passing ships on to the dog-toothed rocks that lined the narrow channel by lighting beacons on either side of the channel, as though there were a clear way between. Then when the ships had struck, the curraghs from Leire's Dun would put out and salvage what they could, in kind or humankind, if the humankind were still living and saleable in any slave market. It was the dear hope of the vil-

lage that one day a ship might run aground without breaking her back, then they would have a vessel that would
let them forage out beyond the islands, where there would
be good pickings from the ships that passed back and
forth with holy relics and church treasures. But alas, no
ship had ever survived the dog-toothed rocks, and so the
pirates of Leire's Dun still relied on their curraghs, long
clumsy shells of tarred cloth or hide, stretched over
wooden frames, able to hold a dozen men, the biggest of
them.

These men were of many kinds, of all races that lived
along the western seaboard of Britain, but most of them
Celtic. They were rough-living, hard-dying scoundrels
to a man who feared nothing, and loved nothing but
gain, come at it how they might. Their chief, Leire, who
bore his great-grandfather's name as a point of primitive

honour, ruled them like beasts of burden, nothing more. He was a massive one-eyed brute himself, almost bald, and with a hunched back as broad as a table top. His men whispered that he was hunched up like that from peering into treasure chests, for it was rumoured that he was extremely rich, though no man dared ask him outright. It was enough to ask him for one's rightful share after a wrecking, let alone pry into his private affairs. But where Leire hid his treasure, no man knew. His house was large and rambling, for he had added to the small original hut that his ancestor had stolen; yet its rooms were empty, but for the haphazard rubbish that a sea-dweller might be expected to accumulate, fishing-nets, oars, benches, and even two comfortable beds, taken from a wrecked ship. Though Leire never slept in a bed himself; he preferred to lie hard on a pile of sacking. Inquisitive men had even searched these beds in his absence, hoping to find his treasure. But the beds held no such secret.

Not that any man would have dared even go into his house, except on piratic business, had he been there. If he had discovered anyone in his house, he would either have killed him outright or have thrown him into the strong-room in the square to howl away his days, without food or water, as a warning to the rest of the village.

But, however strong Leire was, he could not have kept his power in the Dun had he not had a body of cut-throats who were sworn to serve him to the death. These numbered twenty, a pack of blood-thirsty hounds rather than men, the most terrible of whom was Aurog, a monstrous creature, dumb from birth, who thought in his half-witted way that Leire was a god. Aurog never left his master, and tasted all food before Leire dared to eat. It was said that Leire found Aurog on the mountain-side when the monster was a tiny baby and had brought him up as his own. Those who knew of such learned things said that Aurog was more like the Minotaur of Crete than any man should be, except that he didn't have horns on his forehead.

The short curly black wool of his head reached down to his shoulders, and over his chest. His nose was flat and his mouth unnaturally broad, with thick pendulous lips and great jowls that shook when he moved. Once a drunken Pict had removed Aurog's shoes when he was asleep, to see if his feet were of humankind, or cloven hooves. Aurog had awakened and crushed the man to him, breaking his neck. So no one ever knew the truth.

Everyone of Leire's Dun prayed that Aurog would one day meet his match. Many men prayed that Leire himself would find death soon. Yet in spite of this dissension, most of the ruffians who inhabited the hovels on the promontory had to admit in their hearts that Leire had more luck than any other man when it came to luring a ship on to the rocks. He could find a treasure-boat in a barrel of apple cider, they said, and left it at that.

Leire sat in his house, with his bodyguard about him. Aurog gnawed at a beef-bone by his side. Leire, who suffered from an interminable itch, scratched constantly. Now no one noticed it any more, they were so used to it.

Leire had just had great news from the north. A messenger had run in that afternoon, one of a team of relays which Leire kept along the coast, to say that he had heard of a great viking ship that was coming down south between the islands. The man said that it sailed slowly and appeared to carry much weight, and when Leire had asked what emblems the ship bore, the man had said, 'Nothing. It flies a white pennant, but there is nothing carved either at bow or stern.'

'Nothing,' said Leire, scratching. 'Well, out of nothing may come something!' Everyone had forced a laugh at this, except Aurog, who never laughed. He had munched on at his bone.

A strange peace now came upon Thorkell. He understood well enough that Ragnar had taken over control of the *Nameless*, yet he made no mention of it. He seemed to accept it – as he did his blindness – as being inevitable. He did as Harald told him and often the two would sit in the semi-darkness of the aft-cabin, talking for an hour at a stretch, while sometimes Aun, sometimes Horic, sometimes Gnorre would come in for a few moments, when they were not needed in the ship.

Once Thorkell had stood on the aft-platform, sniffing like a blind greyhound, his head held high. Harald was by his side, ready to prevent him from falling if the ship rolled too wildly. Kragge, yarning below with a group of his fellows, looked up and said, 'Look at blind Balder; he has the young spirit of sunlight with him.'

Someone said, 'They might be brothers, from the colour of their hair.'

The name 'Balder' stuck to Thorkell, though it was never said either in his presence or that of Ragnar, who, for all his masterful ways, his cruelty and his treachery, still admitted his blood-brotherhood with Thorkell, and would have thrashed any man who openly insulted Thorkell.

No man could fully understand Ragnar, but once Aun said quietly to Gnorre, 'Yon man is a villain, yet he has certain good qualities that I cannot understand. He will work or starve with us, claiming no privileges. He stole the treasure, yet is ready to share it even with those of us who hate him for his deceit in getting it.'

Gnorre said, 'I hate him, Aun Doorback, yet I too can see some sort of good in him. I think that once he was truly a worthy friend for Thorkell, but that somehow he fell on evil times and became bitter. Now I think that he is a thing of ambition, from his head to his toes. He is all greed – all but a faint shadow of what he was before, that lurks behind his ambition and his greed; and that shadow is his love for Thorkell which has never died fully.'

Aun said, 'I have seen such a thing between brothers. They may quarrel and even do each other a great hurt. Yet underneath there is a strange kind of love for each other. I think I loved my own brother – I certainly wept for him in the dark when no one was there to see – but I believed you did right to kill him, for I knew that he was evil.'

Gnorre said, 'Sometimes we kill the thing we love. Sometimes we see in our brother or even our close friend a part of ourselves. If we kill our friend for evil, we still weep because we have killed a part of ourselves in doing so.'

Wolf Waterhater, who had come up while the two were talking, said, 'You northmen are like old gossips by the chimney fire. You are for ever either killing something or explaining to each other why it should be killed. Can you never leave life and death alone?'

Aun said, 'We are a people not yet born. We are struggling to explain life and death to ourselves. When we all understand what life and death are, then we shall become a united people, like the Romans of old, or the Greeks.'

Wolf said, 'Many folk in Frankland and England and Spain, think you are nothing but savage axemen. They would not believe you if you said such things to them.'

Gnorre said, 'No one will ever give us time to explain. If we put ashore anywhere, immediately men run to meet us and shoot us with arrows. In England, the fierce islanders have even nailed the skins of flayed vikings on their church-doors.'

Aun said, 'Yes, such treatment gives a man no heart to land bearing gifts and sweet words. If you know that they will try to kill you, it is only natural to take an axe and kill them first.'

Wolf began to laugh. 'You are a pair of old hypocrites,' he said, slapping Aun on the back and then rubbing his hand as though he had struck a lump of hard wood. 'I do declare, you had never given a thought to it all till this moment. You have always sailed where you wished and plundered as much as the enemy would allow you!'

When he had gone, Gnorre said, 'Doorback, he doesn't believe a word we have said.'

Aun said, with a twisted smile, 'No. Do you?'

Then they went back to their oars and forgot their talk.

Later Ragnar stood on the forward platform and shouted out, 'Soon we shall pass across the route of the Christ-men. Their ships pass back and forth to Ireland and we may have the good fortune to meet one of them. They are not fighting-men and no doubt we should overcome them easily. Therefore, I say to you now, that if any man in this company has no heart to fight with these long-robed prayer-makers, then him I will excuse. He may take his share of what treasure we find if he will. He need not if his manhood will not let him!'

In the cabin Thorkell said to Harald, 'Ragnar speaks to them fairly, boy. Yet there is no honour in taking a few goblets from old men whose minds are set on their cloisters and their prayers.'

Harald said, 'I have not given much thought to riches. If I had, then I might not worry how they were obtained. At the moment, I wish only to prove myself a warrior so that I can go back proudly to my father. I would not wish to fight a holy man who carried no weapon but his holy book.'

Thorkell placed his white hand on the boy's shoulder. 'I think as you do, Harald, yet it has taken this blindness to make me see more clearly. For a blind man there is no day, no night; it is all one interminable darkness in which he sees only when he is asleep, and they are dreams. And last night I dreamed that a man came to me. I saw him so clearly that at first I thought that it was day and that I had my sight again. This man was dressed in a long gown of rough linen and he wore the top of his head shaven close. He carried a paper in his hand and smiled and then read it, looking up at me from time to time. Then he spoke to me, in Norse, saying, "Thorkell Fairhair, sometimes called 'Skullsplitter,' I have been sent to greet you and to tell you that all will be well with you. There will inevitably be trials, as there must be for all men, but if you are honest with yourself, all will be well." Then he made a mark on the paper he carried, as though he had my name recorded there.'

Harald said, 'What manner of man was he, master? Would you know him again?'

Thorkell smiled and said, 'If I could see him I should. He was of middle height and his face was thin and pale, but patient-looking. I saw that he had a mole by his right nostril. Yes, I would know him again.'

Then he sank so deeply into his own thoughts that Harald left him, going out quietly on to the deck to take his turn at the ship's work.

Just before middle-day, as the *Nameless* skirted a long island that lay low in the sea, they all heard a sound of singing borne to them across the waters from beyond the island. Ragnar's nostrils twitched like those of a hunting-dog and he nodded to his men to hold ready.

The long ship nosed round a rocky tongue of land and then Ragnar ordered the oarbeats to quicken, for immediately ahead of them lay a heavy slow-moving ship. Peering between the shields that were slung round the gunwales, the vikings saw that though this ship bore a square hide sail, she was propelled also by many oarsmen, who sang at their work, for the currents about the island were at variance with the wind, because of the shallow channels wherein the tides turned back upon themselves.

Harald told Thorkell, 'By their long robes and shaven heads, I think these are the men we spoke of earlier.'

Thorkell did not speak, but lay down on the thonged bed and buried his face in the coverings.

The *Nameless* ran swiftly athwart the other ship and then Ragnar ordered that his oarsmen should stay their vessel. The *Nameless* stopped so abruptly that the other ran on and bumped against the longship's side, knocking the oars out of the hands of three vikings, who rubbed their wrists ruefully and swore to have vengeance.

Ragnar stood in the prow and called to a long-robed

man who stood on the platform by the mast of the holy ship. 'What treasure have you aboard?'

The holy man called back in a voice almost as strong, 'Nothing that we have is our own, neither our immortal souls nor anything else, sea wolf. Delay us no longer for we go about our Master's business.'

Ragnar scoffed and said, 'If what you have is not your own, then you will not mind if we take it from you! As for going about your business, that depends on us; we wish to go about our business, and that involves keeping you a little longer.'

The cowled man under the mast said, 'You speak too well to be a fool, so I will ask you again to go your ways and let us do the same. Good journey to you and may God guard you.'

He spoke to his own oarsmen then as though the interview were at an end. This angered Ragnar who leapt aboard the other vessel, to be followed immediately by a score of vikings. Harald saw the grey-robed oarsmen rise from their benches and go to meet the warriors, their sleeves rolled up and their fists clenched. Many of them were great raw-boned men who must have spent more time at the oar than at the altar. One red-faced man with the shoulders of a blacksmith met Kragge and punched the viking so hard beneath the ear that he fell over, carrying Sven and Ottar with him. The Norsemen still in the *Nameless* laughed loud at this and cheered on the big monk, who then looked sorry for what he had done and tried to help them up again. But Kragge, furious at this assault, drew a short knife and ran in on the big oarsman. He flung up his arms and fell to the deck. Aun Doorback clutched his own axe and swore that if he were within reach of Kragge, the man would go headless to Valhalla.

The fight, such as it was, was soon over, for the monks did not pursue their first advantage, and the vikings were not there to play games of courtesy. Soon men were coming back to the *Nameless* with heavy sacks and barrels, calling out to those who still sat aboard that the treasure was worth a better battle than that. Gnorre turned his head away. 'They can take it who will. I want no share of it.' Many others agreed with him, but did not say so openly, as he had done.

At last Ragnar was left alone on the holy vessel. He told the oarsmen that they might go on to wherever they were bound. Their leader said sadly, 'Now that you have taken away our reason for travelling, we have little reason for breaking our backs against the tides. If our entreaties will not touch your hearts to return the property of the Church, we shall return whence we came, sea-thief.'

The last word seemed to nettle Ragnar who turned on the man and said, 'You should be thankful that we have taken only your chalices and salvers, and not your heads and hearts.'

The cowled man said, 'Perhaps you have taken our hearts.'

Ragnar said, 'Then your hearts are trumpery things of gold and silver. I thought that you were of rarer metal than that!'

The man in the cowl said, 'You are not only a common water rogue, you are a blasphemer. If one of your men will give me an axe, I will break a vow and take your head from you. Who offers me an axe?'

No one stirred in the *Nameless*, though Sven said, 'This is a real man, despite his robes.'

Aun turned on him and said, 'What do you know of real men, farmer's boy?' Thereafter Sven and his brothers were silent.

Ragnar, beside himself with rage, shouted, 'Will no one lend this Christ-man an axe, if he wishes to commit suicide?'

The vikings sat mute. Ragnar turned to the *Nameless*. 'Two of you,' he shouted, 'bring this praying beggar aboard. He shall come with us and taste viking mercy at my leisure.'

The cowled monk waved aside the two men who came to fetch him. Their names were Thurgeis and Hageling. They were quiet-natured men, who had no wish to harm the holy man. They allowed him to step aboard the *Nameless* without hindrance. When he stood aboard the longship he turned to his crest-fallen followers and said gently to them, 'Return home, brothers, and pray that these heathens come to God in good time. Do not pray for me, I command you. Good-bye.'

He did not look at them again. He went where he was told and sat on the bench by the mast. The holy ship pulled away and sailed south-westwards then. This time the oarsmen were silent.

Harald noted the cowled monk's bearing and his quiet devotions as the longship set course once more. He turned to Thorkell and said, 'I can understand why they followed this man. He has a strong bearing.'

Thorkell said, 'Is his face thin and pale?'

Harald said, 'Yes, Master.'

Thorkell shuddered a little and then said, 'Can you see his nose? Is there a small mole beside his left nostril?'

Harald watched the man closely, as he raised his head

towards the heavens and his cowl fell back on to his shoulders.

'No, Master,' said the boy. 'The mole is beside the right nostril.'

Thorkell lowered his blind head. 'That is the man I was shown in my dream,' he said. 'Now my fate comes upon me.'

When he had thought the matter over for a while, Thorkell asked Harald to lead him to the holy man. Harald did as he was bid. The man looked up and saw that Thorkell was blind. He rose and took his hands.

'How did your blindness come, my son?' he said gently.

'It came with the wind and the rock-dust on a northern island, Christ-man,' said Thorkell, at first a little angry that the man should call him 'son.'

'Then take care of yourself,' said the monk, 'and God may let you see again, for it is only the outer casing of the eye that is troubled. The precious sight of the eye is still there, but cloaked with pain. It is sometimes the same with a man's spirit; the spirit is good enough, but he has let it become surrounded by disease. The disease of the spirit, and that is more deadly than the disease of the flesh.'

Thorkell made a movement of irritation. 'I did not come to hear a sermon,' he said. 'I hold to other gods than you. I came to say that you shall come to no harm on this ship, if I have the power to prevent it. If you should be sold into slavery, then I promise to buy you from Ragnar, and will turn you free straightaway. You will not be kept against your will once we strike shore.'

The holy man smiled and said, 'Thank you, viking. But it is something which you must decide. I am content, whatever God asks me to tolerate. I will only tell you that this is, in its way, a joyful meeting for me.'

Thorkell broke in scornfully, 'Joyful? To be held captive by men you do not know or love?'

The monk said softly, 'But I do know you. I saw you in a dream I had but last night. I saw the very bandage about your eyes, and in my dream you told me that the cruel winds of Orkney had blinded you. That is why I asked but now – and you gave me the self-same answer. Then I knew that I was sent to you with a purpose.'

Thorkell clapped his hands to his bandages, as though he would tear them off. But the fit passed and his hands fell again. He turned from the monk and said, half to himself, 'So we met in our dreams, the two of us. It was meant to be, all this. Now I know the answer to one thing at least, that there is another world, another life, beyond that which we know waking.'

He walked back slowly to the cabin, no longer leaning on Harald's shoulder. It was as though he had found direction, blind as he was. To Harald it seemed that Thorkell had grown older, much older, in that last hour.

When night fell, the *Nameless* was still ploughing a southerly course. She was among the narrows between the smaller islands before Rolf realized it, for he had never navigated this stretch before. Then they all were concerned to hear not only the dull booming of surf on both sides of them, but the vicious rushing of water about some rocky outcrops before them.

Sven said, 'We should have made landfall earlier, while there was still light to see by. This is a shallow, treacherous sea, I have heard.'

Even as he spoke a beacon flared up to their left. Then, almost within a breath of the first, another to their right. Gnorre said, 'Praise Odin, now we may steer through the channel between the rocks.'

Within the pull of five oars later, the *Nameless* shuddered in every timber, then groaned, and then gave a great heave like a stag when the spear probes deep, and turned half-about, her deck tilting so high and violently that men fell hither and thither, sliding down towards the frothing breakers that now ringed the longship.

Thorkell gave a great cry, as though of agony, and stumbled out from the cabin, tearing off his bandages in a vain effort to see. Aun ran and grasped him, then clutched hard to the mast so as to save him from being swept overboard by the great waves that washed the doomed vessel. But for her loose keel, the *Nameless* would have broken her back there and then. As it was, she took the violence of the first shock, then pitched sideways and filled almost straightway and began to settle. At the least a dozen vikings were thrown into the darkness and went swirling away to their deaths, silently, as though they had never been.

Then the longship settled, heeled half-over, and men the vikings did not know were scrambling over her like flies about a meat-bone. They were laughing and shouting to each other joyously. Some carried torches, and by their light the vikings saw that these men had come out in long tarred curraghs.

Harald tried to draw his sword, but a great skin-clad man clubbed him viciously at the side of the head. As the boy fell, he saw Aun shielding Thorkell from the assault and trying in vain to reach out for the axe which Gnorre offered him. Then as Harald lost consciousness, he saw Gnorre fall face downwards, and the axe flying from his hand and over the side of the longship.

The score of vikings who had survived the wreck lay on the damp earthen floor of Leire's strong-room. Leire looked down at them from the stone steps that led to the street above. Aurog was behind him, slavering like an animal. Leire said harshly, 'Which is your leader?'

At first no one stirred, for the vikings had been cruelly treated on their march up the stony pathway from the sea. Then Ragnar raised himself on his elbow and pointed to Thorkell. 'That is our shipmaster, man. But as you see he is too sick to be meddled with. I am his second and will take on my shoulders what you may ask.'

Aun said to Horic, 'He has some good in him, after all.' But Horic's head only swayed weakly, as though he were too far gone to understand the words spoken to him. Gnorre lay between the two, his eyes closed and his face twisted with pain from the great club wound at the back of his head.

Leire smiled down at blind Thorkell, who sat with his hands clasped about his knees, his head sunk. 'I shall regard the blind one as your leader,' he said. 'He will be responsible in my eyes for whatever you shall do.'

Then he went out and a short while later two men came armed with spears and flung pieces of smoked meat into the dungeon. The vikings ignored it, though the monk, who was still with them took up a piece and ate a little of it. 'Forgive me, friends,' he said, 'but I have been fasting for three days and now I must eat or I shall lack strength should I need it.'

No one heeded his words, so he munched on silently. At last he went to Harald, who lay beside Thorkell, staring up at the little square of window that stood at street level.

'Try to eat something, my son,' he said. 'You must keep strength in your body. God would wish you to make the best of this adventure.'

He smiled as he offered the lad a piece of the meat. Harald overcame his repugnance at the sight of it and tried to do as he was told.

The day passed slowly. Men spoke little except to ask how their friends had died. Rolf Wryneck was among the dead. By some fatal irony, his neck had been broken with the first shock of the wreck, for he stayed at his steerboard till the last, trying to steer away from that awful rushing water. The fate he had escaped five years before had now come on him again, when no man thought it would.

Ottar, the son of Olaf and Asa, was dead too. He had died bravely, trying to fight with the wreckers, barehanded. His two brothers, Sven and Rollo, still lived, but their cousins were among those swept overboard in the first rush of the sea over the gunwales.

Harald gazed up at Thorkell's hopeless face and wished that he had the words to comfort him. But Thorkell was beyond consolation for the time being. He had spoken but once, and that was to ask if the *Nameless* was a wreck. When he had heard that her ribs were stove in on one side, he had laughed and said, 'Thank Odin that he has, prevented this rabble from sailing her.'

Then he fell silent and brooding and had not spoken again.

As darkness came on, men came with small clay lamps, filled with oil and burning twisted hemp for a wick. Others brought in two pannikins of water. They all waited until Thorkell had wet his lips before they drank. The monk was given his share like the rest and the pannikin handed to him with a certain respect. His bearing throughout the day had impressed them all, though they would not have admitted to this weakness.

When he had drunk, Ragnar came to Thorkell and took him by the hand, kneeling before him. 'I ask forgiveness, brother,' he said. 'It was my evil-doing that brought this disaster upon us all.'

Thorkell's lips twisted for a while, trying to speak. Then he said softly, 'Get up from your knees, Raven. Kneel to no man, brother. If you have been a fool, then you have been a fool – but that is no reason to kneel! In any case, I know now that this would have come upon us whatever we had done.'

He took Ragnar's hand and pressed it. Ragnar turned from him then for the tears were beginning to run down his gaunt and swarthy cheeks. 'I shall repay your kindness, Thorkell,' he said.

'Whatever you say, you will never become Ragnar Dove,' said Thorkell; 'it will always be Ragnar Raven.'

'They understand each other,' said the monk to Aun. Aun nodded. 'They are not saints, Christ-man,' he said, 'yet there is a strange good in them both, if a man will only try to look for it.' The monk said, 'Yes, so is it with all men, my son.'

Aun said, 'If you call me son, must I then call you

father?' He was already laughing, in his old jesting way. The monk laughed too. 'No,' he said. 'Your father was a bear from the forests! No, you can call me John, if you choose, for that is my name.'

'John! John! John!' said Aun, trying the name over on his tongue. Then he nodded, 'Very well, John,' he said. 'That is what I shall call you.'

Towards night, Ragnar made a man hold a blanket over the window-hole so that none of the folk outside should see them. Then he called the others into a circle and said, 'Vikings if we stay here we shall grow weak and lose heart. If we are to escape from this dungeon, it must be soon. When shall it be?'

There was some argument, then Rollo said, 'I say that we should go at dawn time. That would give us time to sleep and refresh ourselves.'

Ragnar slapped him on the shoulder and said, 'That was in my own mind too, young viking. Now, say on, Rollo, and how shall we go from here?'

Rollo said, 'I have tried the window bars and they are too strong for a man to move them. There is an archway of stone in the wall behind you, but that is shored up with stout planks of wood and will lead nowhere. The only way is through the door at the top of the steps and into the street.'

Ragnar said, with a slight sneer, 'Have you set your back against that door, Rollo?'

Rollo nodded his head. 'It is a good three inches thick, Master,' he said. 'I felt it with my finger and thumb as they dragged me in.'

Ragnar said, 'Then how shall we go through that door, friend?'

And Rollo scratched his head, defeated. Ragnar said then with a smile, 'Well, what muscle cannot do, guile must. I will open the door at dawn, and be you all still as mice in the thatch at winter-time.'

He stood up then and said, 'How many will come with me?'

Most of the vikings put up their hands to show their willingness. Those who did not were Thorkell, Wolf Waterhater, Harald, Horic, Aun Doorback and Gnorre Nithing. The monk stood with his arms folded. He did not join in the discussion at all.

When they had decided that they would escape at dawn, the vikings became more jovial, for it was as though a weight had been lifted from their minds by the decision to take action.

Now men began to hammer on the door and call for meat and wine. Ragnar pushed a gold coin that had not been stolen from him under the door and soon one of the guard brought in a wooden platter of bread and smoked fish and a great stone jar of a rough-tasting mead.

'You robber,' shouted Ragnar, in pretended rage. 'You have cheated me, bringing only the orts from another's table, in return for a true gold piece.'

The man shrugged and grinned, presenting his keen spearpoint at Ragnar when he moved towards him. Ragnar saw three more men standing behind the guard, in the narrow doorway, their axes ready. He made no further demur and the door was shut once more.

'We shall need much good luck at dawn,' he said with a grim smile. 'It is a narrow place and one man could hold it against twenty, if he were armed and they barehanded. Well, we shall see.'

Those who were planning to escape sat about the meat and wine and made themselves a feast. Though the others were invited to join them, they did not do so for there was little enough food and drink, and those who were going at dawn would need as much sustenance as they could get.

Only Thorkell sat with them for a moment or two and drank from Ragnar's clay cup to wish him luck. There were fourteen of them, all strong men, most of them scarred in many battles. Yet now they seemed innocent and young in Harald's eyes, as though they were untried boys about to perform an act of dedication. In the flickering light of the little lamps, their eyes were bright and anxious, and looked up at Ragnar when he spoke, as though he knew the secret of eternal life.

Aun turned away, his head down. He wished that he were making the attempt with them, but he could not leave Thorkell. A blind man could not make such a hazardous attempt, for he would endanger the safety of the others. That had been understood by them all from the start.

Now the feasters became merry and called on Horic to amuse them before they lay down to rest. He stood in the torchlight with a little pebble in his hand, on his flat palm for all to see. 'Watch the mouse,' he said, and swiftly waved his other hand over the pebble.

The vikings saw the long tail and the grey fur and the bright beads of eyes as the tiny creature held up its head and wrinkled its nose.

Aun said to the monk, 'What think you of that, John?'

The monk smiled and said, 'That is wonderful.' But to

him the stone had never changed, though he knew that the vikings had seen a mouse.

Horic passed his hand over the mouse again and it had gone. The vikings cheered him and shouted, 'Another trick, Horic! Another one before we go!'

Horic took out his length of twine. It dangled from his fingers. 'This twig will flower,' he said. All men but the monk saw the twine stiffen and then climb upwards in his fingers until it stuck up as straight as a twig.

Yet at that moment a man outside the window coughed and a woman in the street laughed out raucously. Horic shuddered and the twig fell, to become a length of twine once more. He turned to the vikings and said, 'The magic has gone out of me. It will not come again tonight.'

Then the vikings shook hands with each other and many of them kissed Thorkell as though they were going on a long journey and would wish an older brother farewell. He did not speak to them, but the tears ran down his face unhindered.

Then Ragnar blew out the lamps and the vikings made themselves as comfortable as they could, those who were going with Ragnar in one group, those who were to stay behind in another.

In the darkness Ragnar went to Thorkell and put his arms round his neck lovingly. 'Good-bye, brother,' he said. 'When I hated you most, I loved you most.'

Thorkell said, 'In Valhalla there will be no more hate, only love. There you shall tell me of this escape.'

Then they parted and were silent, though no man slept much that night.

When the dawn came and the chill winds blew into the dungeon, Harald raised himself on his elbow and waited. Ragnar rose silently and went to the door. He peered a while through the great keyhole and then whispered, 'Guard! Hey, guard!'

At length, Harald heard the shuffling of feet outside and the sound of a smothered yawn. Ragnar turned to those in the room and put his finger over his lips.

'Guard,' he said again, through the keyhole. 'Are you listening to me? Harken then, there is one in this place who wears a necklace of gold that would buy a man twenty horses. He lies asleep now near my feet.'

The guard mumbled sleepily for a moment and then made a slight exclamation of surprise. Ragnar sensed his growing interest and said, 'He lies ready for the plucking, warrior. He is an old enemy of mine and I tell you because I would pay back old scores. If you wish for a fortune, then it is yours, but you must take it with your own hands for I dare not touch him. I am afraid of him.'

Ragnar waited long then and it seemed to them all that the trick would not work. The man outside moved away from the door as though he were listening for something. All in the room lay still, scarcely breathing. Then Ragnar said, 'If you tell others, they will share it. If you take it, it will be yours alone – and you will bring vengeance on my enemy for me.'

Ragnar lay on the top step, a smile on his face that was not good to see. Harald shivered to see the thin lips almost bitten through by the strong white teeth.

Then the door began to creak slightly and, in the uncertain light of the early dawn, began to move. Ragnar moved back with it, so as not to be seen. When it was open a foot wide, the man peered forward, a rough sword in his hand. Still Ragnar did not move. The guard leaned, so as

to see the man who lay near the foot of the steps, as Ragnar had said. As he did so, Ragnar suddenly sprang into
life, and with a cruel lunge, slammed the thick oaken
door hard on the man and his weapon. The head and
sword-arm were trapped as in a vice. The man had only
time to give a sharp gasp when Ragnar had struck him
with clenched fist hard on the temples, and the sword fell
into the dungeon from the unclenched hand. Then Ragnar swung open the door and the man dropped down the
steps, limp as a pennant drenched in a heavy sea.

Ragnar stooped to pick up the sword. He spared a
glance at the man and smiled grimly. Rollo went over
and lifted the man's head by the hair then let it fall. With
that one blow Ragnar had broken his neck. The vikings
smiled and rubbed their hands together in admiration.
They would have cheered had they been able.

Harald did not dare watch them go through the door.
When he looked up again they had gone. Aun was staring at the closed door, his fists clenching and unclenching.

At length he rose and opened the door cautiously. Then
he bundled the dead guard outside and shut the door
again. Thorkell, his red eyes still closed, whispered, 'That
was well done, friend.'

It seemed that day would never come. The dawn lingered over Leire's Dun as though wishing to torment the waiting vikings in the dungeon. They lay with closed eyes, listening, but for a while all that they heard were the cries of swooping gulls above the village roofs, and the distant thudding of the sea on the rocky shore.

At length they heard footsteps outside their door and an exclamation of surprise; then the feet running away, and others coming. A head looked in at the window hole for an instant, then the great key turned in the lock again.

'They have discovered the dead guard and have found that our comrades have escaped,' said Horic. Aun only nodded. He sat holding Gnorre's cold hand, speechless with grief.

No one came to bring them food that morning. Footsteps and quiet whispering voices sounded in the street. There was a strange tension everywhere. It seemed as though folk wanted to laugh uproariously, or cry out loudly, yet held back those sounds.

Thorkell stopped rocking backwards and forwards and said, 'I do not like it. I thought they would have come to us here, to find out what they could about the escapers. They are leaving us alone, deliberately.'

The monk John kneeled in a corner and prayed quietly.

Harald, his nerves on edge with waiting, walked round

the low dungeon, examining the walls, to give his mind something to bite on. He stopped by the archway at the back of the room; it was blocked in by thick planks of oak. Yet there were interstices between the boards. Harald felt a cold air sweep through them to his face. He peered through the cracks, but could see nothing. Yet it seemed to him that a distant low booming came up from behind that door. He told Horic, who said, after he too had listened, 'That is the sea.'

The others came and listened and Thorkell said, 'Doubtless there is a long tunnelway behind these planks, which comes out above the shore somewhere. It would need a giant's strength to move these great pieces of wood, though, for they are sunk into the ground and wedged hard at the top of the archway. Could you move them, Aun?'

Aun Doorback let go Gnorre's hand and moved slowly to the door. He tested it with all his strength, and said at last, 'If I were rested and had good food inside me, I might move a plank or two. But my strength has gone from me since the wreck, Thorkell.'

He went back to his dead friend and sat silent. John knelt in the corner and prayed again. Harald began to bite at his fingernails. The time must have been midday.

'They have great faith in their planks,' said Thorkell.

'Either that or the mouth of the tunnel is guarded,' said Horic. 'Or perhaps it comes out high above the sea.'

'Are you hoping to escape, Thorkell?' said Aun, moving his eyes slowly towards the leader.

Thorkell passed his hand across his eyes and said, 'Perhaps. Perhaps I might not be a drag on you if we could get out from this place.' He said no more, but sank his head again in his hands and brooded for a while.

Suddenly wild horns skirled in the village and skin drums began to throb in a strange savage rhythm. All in the cell looked up. Then Harald went to the high window and jumped up so as to see outside. He shrank back with a sudden cry for he had seen a hand, a white hand, resting at street level, just outside the window. He did not see the arm or the body – just the hand, and it was still.

He gave a gasp and turned to tell someone of this, when the door burst open and without warning the dungeon seemed to be full of wild-eyed villagers, who jostled with each other to get at the captive vikings. In less time than it would take for a man to count twenty, the tribesmen had bound their prisoners by the wrists and were dragging them up the steps towards the street.

Outside, the vikings blinked in the bright light. They saw the mud hovels, the thatched roofs, the small square teeming with shouting folk. Above them the sea-birds shrieked as though to be in company with the savage inhabitants of Leire's Dun.

Harald, who walked next to John, turned his head as soon as he got into the street towards the window of the cell. Sven was lying there, an arrow in his chest, his arm flung out so that his hand lay by the side of the window. The vikings saw this and gasped. Then they looked towards the centre of the square where the greatest shouting was to be heard. A heap of bodies lay tumbled on each other – Kragge, Thurgeis, Rollo, and all the rest, man for man, each one pierced by an arrow. Ragnar lay on the top of the heap of dead. His eyes were rolled back and his teeth bared in a savage grin. In his right hand he still clutched a long thick tress of black hair. Three arrows pierced his breast, their broken shafts hanging down as though he had tried to tear them out.

Thorkell said, 'Why are you so stricken, vikings? What can you see?'

No one would tell him, but at last John whispered to him, 'Thorkell, my son, your comrades who went from the dungeon have met disaster. They lie dead before us.'

Thorkell said, 'Is Ragnar with them?'

John said, 'Yes, viking. He died a brave death. All his wounds are at the front.'

Thorkell said, 'You speak well, John, for a priest. You would have made a good warrior with a little teaching.'

John said, 'I am a warrior in my way, I thank God. I will say a prayer for our dead.'

Thorkell noticed that now he said 'our' as though he was one of the viking band. Thorkell smiled and said, 'I cannot think that your God would approve of your new alliance, John, but no doubt it will do no harm. At least *they* all know the answer now. . . .'

He said no more, but allowed Leire's tribesmen to lead him to the whipping-posts that were set where the crowd was thickest. Each viking was bound to a stout pine stump, his hands above his head. Those who still wore shirts had them torn away. Even the monk's vestment was ripped down. Harald saw that his back was hard and muscular. The crowd jeered and hooted them. Aun's back was laid bare and the tattooed dragon was exposed to view.

'I will make that beast writhe for mercy,' said a great savage, whose matted hair almost hid his face. He twirled a heavy whip with many weighted thongs. It hissed in the air like a family of vipers, suddenly awakened from their sleep.

Aun said, 'It would need a better man than you, ape-man.'

The whipman spat at Aun in his rage. Aun merely smiled and shrugged his broad shoulders.

John, bound next to Harald, whispered with a smile, 'Have courage, boy. The pain of the body soon passes. It is the pain of the spirit that hurts. If your spirit is strong, then slave body will obey it and will bear the pain. I shall pray for you.'

Harald thanked him. Then Leire stood on the roof of a low hovel and taunted them. He told them that they must pay for the disobedience of their fellows. Especially must they pay for the death of Aurog, his dear friend, whom Ragnar had throttled while the arrows were still in him.

Thorkell spoke up then and said, 'We are willing to pay Ragnar's debt, then, pig-face, for he would have paid ours. Only I ask you to spare the boy and the priest. They are not to blame for anything.'

Leire said, 'You must all taste the mercy of Leire, my friends.' He was angry that Thorkell should have insulted him, for he could see that many among the crowd enjoyed the viking's taunt.

Thorkell said, 'Stay, snout! I am the leader of this band. I will take the whipping for them all. Is that a good bargain?'

Aun said, 'That you shall not, Fairhair. I am as good a man as you.'

Leire said, 'Hark at them, these seacocks, they even quarrel about who shall die first! Nay, nay, blind one, all will be beaten.'

Thorkell said, 'As well ask a mangy wolf for the bone he gnaws. Well, trough-grubber, I make you a last offer – do not let the bargain pass, it will not be offered again. Look, I am a blind man, but I will fight you, or any warrior you have that dares meet me, but let these others go back untouched to their prison.'

Aun shouted, 'Why should you have the pleasure, Thorkell? Look, midden-grunter, I will fight any two men you have, yourself included, if you count yourself as a man!'

At this the crowd yelled with joy at the viking's bravado. Leire's sullen face flushed. He shouted to the whippers, who rushed in and began to wield their vicious flails.

Aun was still yelling taunts at Leire when the man who whipped him staggered with exhaustion. Now the crowd was silent and breathless. The dragon that had once circled the great viking's back had disappeared.

At last Leire said, 'Enough! There is always another day.'

The whippers wiped the sweat from their faces and bodies, thankful to rest.

The square was empty now. Only the sea-birds still wheeled above it as the afternoon sun began to sink in the west.

The dungeon was twilit when Harald came to his senses again. At first he wondered where he was. Then he saw Horic bending over him and he remembered. Horic said, 'Your back – does it hurt, boy?' Harald sat up and shrugged his shoulders. Then he gave a wry grimace but did not answer. Horic said, 'You were lucky. They were merciful to you because of your youth. They dealt quite kindly with the priest too, though he begged them not to.'

Harald looked round the cell. Aun was lying in the corner, muttering terribly to himself. His face was drawn and horrible to see. He looked more like a vengeful fury than a man. The others did not go near him at that time. John came across to the boy when he saw that he had awakened. He smiled down and put his hand on Harald's shoulder gently. 'God be praised,' he said, 'for He has given Thorkell back his sight. When the first lash fell, so great was Thorkell's rage that he went berserk, and the scales fell from his eyes with wrath, and he sees again now ! Look at him !'

Thorkell was standing, his back all bloody, but his head erect, by the high window. Wolf was by his side. They were talking in an undertone together. Now they seemed as they were when Harald first met them on the shores of the fjord, two close friends, with no Ragnar to come between them. Wolf seemed happy, as though even his tortured back was worth having if it brought Thorkell's friendship with it.

Horic said, 'Sometimes suffering brings a reward with it.'

Aun looked at him, then at poor Gnorre's body which still lay in the corner, and growled menacingly. John said, 'Aun is taking it all very hard. But he will recover. He is as resilient as a tough old oak tree.'

Thorkell turned then, and though Harald saw that his young face was lined and begrimed, he was smiling. He came across to the boy and said, 'Well borne, viking! I will give you another sword one day, if we ever reach our fjord again.'

Then he went across the cell and spoke to Aun, at first gently, then almost harshly. Aun recognized the voice of his master and stopped growling like a wild beast. Wolf joined them. Harald sensed that they were planning to escape, and now the heart of each of them was bitter against his captivity. Better to die, thought Harald, than live such a life. The face of the monk, John, had lost some of its gentleness and was set in firmer, more warrior-like lines. But for his cropped hair, it would have been hard to recognize him as a religious man, for his habit was now torn and hanging about him, only held to his body by its stout rope girdle.

That night no food was put into their cell. They had therefore been almost twenty-four hours without breaking their fast. Nor were they given lamps that night.

Thorkell said grimly, 'Well, we can work as well in the dark, can we not, Aun?'

Aun said, 'We must find a flint or two from the floor of the cell, if we are to dig, then it matters not whether we have light or not. We can feel to dig, like the mole.'

Thorkell said, 'I have become so used to the dark that I am not troubled.'

So, while they could still see in the twilight, they grubbed up a few long flints from the earthen floor of the dungeon, and having chosen the sharpest, sat down to wait for night to come. There was much to do and they knew they must waste no time.

When it became so dusk that none could see into the dungeon from the street, they began to scrape away the hard-trodden earth at the base of the arched doorway. It was a mighty task for men whose strength had been sapped by privation and punishment, yet they worked on and on, for they knew that their lives hung on this effort.

As one tired, so another took his place, Harald working as hard as the rest of them, until after two hours of scraping and digging, they had got down almost to the base of the deep-sunk planks that blocked the archway. Once, as they dug, footsteps had sounded outside their door, and for a while they had lain silent, until the steps had gone away again. Then they worked more feverishly than before, to make up for the time they had lost.

At length, when the first of the grey flickers of dawn began to creep over the eastern seas, they had moved the earth away so that the planks might be swung outwards into the dungeon to let them pass into the far tunnel. Then they stopped and each shook hands with the other solemnly.

'We must keep together while we can,' said Thorkell, 'yet if one of us lags, the others must leave him, or we shall all die. Leire would not tolerate another escape.'

John kneeled down in his corner and said a prayer for

them all. He stayed a while by Gnorre's body, though Aun pushed him away a little too roughly. 'This is not your concern, Christ-man,' he said, 'let Gnorre go to his own gods. Do not meddle.' John forgave Aun, for he knew how much the great viking had loved the dead outlaw. He smiled up at Aun's wrathful face and went to join Thorkell.

Then they began to move the planks, each man straining with all his might, for it seemed that they had been sunk in the earth for many years. When they moved the first, a small trickle of earth and stones began to fall into the dungeon. When they had moved the second, that trickle became a stream, and now the very archway began to tremble.

Thorkell said, 'Stand back, or we shall be buried. That archway is ready to fall. Those planks have held up the whole side of this dungeon.'

But as yet the space was only big enough to let Harald pass through into the tunnel. Suddenly Aun pushed forward and stood in the archway, holding up his hands and taking the weight of the structure on his broad and mutilated shoulders. Harald saw the pain it caused him to touch the rough stonework, but the viking's face was set. His voice was now hoarse and commanding. 'Move the third plank, you fools,' he said. 'I cannot wait here for ever. Move it and pass through. I will follow.'

Thorkell said, 'It is madness, Aun, for once the third support has gone, you will be left with the whole weight of the rock wall on your back.'

Aun stared into his master's eyes sternly. 'Do as I say, young man,' he commanded. 'Do you not recall my eke-name?'

'Aun Doorback,' said Horic; 'but you are truly named.'
Then they swung the third plank away and passed
through into the tunnel as fast as they might. As Thorkell went through last, a shower of big stones fell about
his head, and above them there was the awful sound of
rock, straining against rock, an immense subterranean tension, like the creaking of a gigantic door of stone.

Thorkell heard this. He heard Aun's deep and laboured
breathing as his great thews and sinews stretched and
almost broke beneath the titanic strain.

'Come with us now, Aun, or it will be too late,' he
said.

Aun only cursed at him, telling him to go away.
Harald saw that the man's eyes were closed and that
his face worked with a dreadful spasm. The priest, John,
went to Aun and prayed beside him. Aun's eyes opened
wide and rolled horribly. The foam was now flecking his
lips. He used his last breath to shout, 'Go, all of you, or
may Odin's ravens peck out your eyes! I can hold it no
longer.'

Thorkell said, weeping, 'Aun, beloved warrior, come
with us. We will all hold up the roof while you get from
under it.'

Aun spat at him and whispered, 'I stay with Gnorre.'

Then there was a fearful grinding of rock above them
and the very floor beneath their feet seemed to shake in
sympathy. Thorkell led them away from the doorway
and into the passageway. As they stepped back the rock
fell, massive, stirring up clouds of dry dust. Aun's great
scarred hand stuck out from between the immense
boulders that fell. Nothing more of him could be seen.
The great hand clenched and then unclenched. It lay

still. Thorkell bent and kissed the gnarled fingers. Then as other rocks began to fall about them, they turned and made off, bent double, along the passage, towards the sound of the booming surf.

As they ran on that nightmare journey along the twisting tunnel, the light filtered through to them gradually
and the sound of the sea became clearer and clearer.
Once they passed through a great cavern, where the tunnel widened out suddenly, to give on to this broad space,
from the roof of which hung strange growths of weed,
and the floor of which was deep in ancient shells, the
fossilized remains of a much earlier world. Then they
had passed through the green gloom of the cave to the
tunnel again, though now it became much wider and
higher, and they were able to run without bending low.

Harald gasped, 'That would be a fine place to hide
one's treasure.'

They all laughed, in spite of themselves, that the boy
should be thinking of treasure at such a time.

'Perhaps Leire does,' said Wolf Waterhater, stumbling
on, his hand clapped to his side, for he suffered from a
painful stitch.

Then, suddenly the light came full into their faces
as they turned a sharp corner, and they stood out on a
platform of rock above the sea.

As Thorkell came to the entrance of the passage-way,
he stopped short and gave a great gasp, his finger pointing below them and to their right. They all followed his
gaze.

On a rocky shoal, between two long, dog-toothed ridges

on which the sea broke in a foamy spray, lay the *Name-less*. Her mast was shattered and her mainsail dragged with the tides. She lay on her side, the waves breaking over her, the currents flowing through her broken sides. The vikings drew in their breath, in compassion for their ruined longship.

Thorkell wiped his hand across his face. 'Well, at least we know the end of her,' he said sadly. 'None of those land-rats will ever sail in her now!'

Then he turned his head and they all looked below them. The rock fell steeply from the cavern, but not too steeply for men who had already braved so much. Far beneath them lay a strip of sand, and pulled up on to it, three or four curraghs of different sizes.

'That is our goal,' said Thorkell, as he leapt down the rocky slope. The others followed, now careless of life or limb. The cold dawn air chilled them but set their blood tingling. They were filled with a strange excitement. The smell of the sea, strong and heady, made them drunk. They shouted a war-cry as they leapt.

Then from above and behind them they heard another shout. Horic, who was last in the line, turned and stopped for an instant. He saw a tall dark shape on the rocky hilltop above the passage-way. It was one of Leire's guards. Horic saw him thrust out one arm and draw back the other. He ducked, expecting to hear the arrow whizz over his head. It struck him between the shoulder blades. He flung up his arms and with a high cry, pitched forward, to fall before the others. He rolled quickly down the slope, taking with him a runnel of pebbles. Thorkell stopped for a moment as Horic's body struck the sharp rocks below. 'He was dead before he reached the beach,' he said. 'Crouch low and run for your lives. We must not stop now.'

Once an arrow whirred above them. Once a shaft glanced on the very rock where Harald had leaned a second or two before and shattered itself to pieces, flying on through the brightening air with the vicious sound of a hornet.

Then, sobbing and gasping, they reached the beach, and staggered over its soft surface towards the tarred curraghs.

They lay unguarded, their paddle-oars stacked beside them. Thorkell and Wolf rocked one of them, the smallest, until it was clear of the clogging sand, and then all pushed the flimsy shell to where the breakers ran in on to the pebbles. John and Harald carried four oars. They clambered into the curragh while the others pushed on until they were waist deep. Wolf groaned with pain as the salt water bit into his raw back, but still he pushed.

Then Thorkell yelled, 'Aboard, Wolf, the tide will take her now.' First one, then the other, scrambled into the curragh. The light shell seemed to shudder with their weight. A flurry of waters struck her and for a moment she hung, turning back towards the shore. The four rowers worked like souls damned to bring her out to the current again.

At last she swung free of the shore and began to move out of the shallow channel where the *Nameless* lay, and so beyond the far ridge of rocks, into the open sea. Now their spirits lifted, despite the great sadness of their lost comrades. For a while they sang wordless songs, out of the bursting fullness of their tormented hearts.

And so singing and weeping and rowing they passed

out of sight of the rocky coast on which lay Leire's Dun. It was only when they met the great untamed rollers of the ocean that they came to their senses and realized that they had no water, no food, little clothing. Then they remembered their wounds, their weakness, their madness at leaving the land behind them with so little preparation for a voyage.

Wolf said, 'We had little luck with the ship we named *Nameless*. What shall we name this one, shipmaster?'

Thorkell smiled grimly and said, 'I have learned that a ship lives up to its name. Nothing comes of nothing. Very well, then; let this be *Landfinder*. And I pray to Odin that she finds us a good shore to land on before long.'

Wolf said nothing, but from his look as he lowered his head, Harald saw that he had little faith in that prayer. Harald turned to John. The monk's eyes were closed, but his lips were moving in syllables which the boy did not understand. Yet the monk rowed as steadily and as strongly as did Thorkell himself.

Perhaps there is some hope, thought the boy, when he saw this.

A gannet flying low seemed to say, 'Perhaps ... Perhaps.'

The three days since they had taken to the sea again had been days of steadily growing despair. Now the battered curragh lay, almost water-logged, at the mercy of the sea. Three of the paddles had been swept from nerveless hands and had floated away beyond all chance of recovery. As Wolf's had gone, he had said, ironical with exhaustion, 'Good-bye, dear friend, and may we never meet again!'

Then he had burst into loud laughter which had weakened him so much that Thorkell had been forced to turn and strike him across the face to save his reason.

John still had an oar and he pushed this way and pulled that way, more to give himself something to do than with any hope that his puny efforts would change the course of the curragh.

Harald sat, over the knees in water, his hands on his thighs, staring at the bottom of the tarred craft. The sky was dark above them now, and the great grey-green waves rose mercilessly higher and higher about them. Sometimes they lay deep in a twilit trough; sometimes, with a sudden frightening swing, they climbed effortlessly to the summit, and the waters rushed past them as they rose, sickeningly powerful.

Harald tried to remember what his father looked like. But found that the image would not come to his mind now. He tried to recall the name of the old headman in

the village on the fjord, but that eluded him too. There was nothing to think about. Even the man he had killed no longer seemed frightening. The boy tried to make up a song and was actually singing its first harsh note when between his feet, the floor of the curragh split, and a spar of splintered wood appeared as though from nowhere, ripping its way through the flimsy shell, and striking violently on the lad's legs, numbing them with the great force of the blow.

Almost immediately the crazy vessel sank beneath them. They were sitting down upon the waves at one moment, then they were standing in the great waters without any warning.

No one spoke, but each grasped the wooden rim of the waterlogged craft. They stared through each other, seeing nothing but the surging mountains of water, their teeth already chattering with the shock of the sudden immersion.

Then Thorkell came out of his trance and said, 'Ragnar.' It was merely that one word, spoken so softly that Harald only just heard it. He did not look at Thorkell's face. He only saw the red hands slowly unclench on the rocking shell and then disappear. It was some time before Harald understood that Thorkell had gone. He did not feel sorry. He did not feel anything. It was as though only his own hands existed now. There was no sensation in the rest of his body. He began to wonder with what part of him he could see, or think, or hear. He knew only his own hands, chafed raw and cramped. As he looked at them he saw that the ends of his fingers had gone white, very white, down to the first knuckle joint. He wondered why that was. Then he heard Wolf shout out, 'Where has Thorkell gone?' As though Thorkell had walked out of the feast hall without saying where he was going.

John looked towards the swaying breakers. Wolf understood what he meant. He gave a hoarse cry and loosed his grip on the curragh. He had disappeared as soon as his hands let go.

Harald looked at his fingers again. They were white now to the second joint. Then to the hand itself. He watched his fingers loosing the rim of the curragh. The waters swept in at his mouth and he gave up trying to breathe. He began to slip away from the curragh.

Then John clasped him and brought him back again, holding him between his own two weakening arms. A curious gull swept above them, almost alighting on the curragh to see what they were. But at that moment John raised his head and the timid bird swept on up again, into the salt-laden air.

The bird wakened Harald once more. He saw the white flash of its wings, that almost touched his face as it rose, screaming away from them. The bird's cry stirred the boy's memory to life again. He now saw Gudröd's hall clearly again with the flames licking round it, reflected in the dark tarn; he saw the deep forests through which he had trudged with his father; he saw the village nestling by the fjord. Then he saw his father's face. He remembered it now. It came closer and closer to him, bigger and bigger. Now it was very near his own. At first it towered over him, then it came down and down, until it almost touched him. He saw the hair, the eyes, the mouth, all separately, then all blurred.

He heard his father's voice. It said, 'Steady with him. He had almost gone. Lift him aboard. Gently, gently, Rurik! The lad isn't made of iron.'

Then Harald saw that it was not his father after all. Suddenly he felt unsafe. 'John! John! Where is John?' he shouted.

The Danes looked over the side of their longship. They saw only the swirling wastes of water. Their fat, dark-haired shipmaster rubbed his chin. Then he went to where the boy lay, wrapped round with woollen blankets. 'Sleep now, lad,' he said, 'John is with you, John is well.'

Harald smiled and tried to put out his hand. 'Good John,' he said. 'Where is he?'

His hand had moved but a few inches when the boy sank into an unconsciousness as deep as the sea he had been saved from.

The shipmaster said, 'There will be time enough when he is well again to tell him that there was no John there when we found him.'

Indeed, of all the longship's crew, Harald was now the only one left. John had held him afloat just long enough for the Danish ship to sight him and then, his work finished, had slipped beneath the waves.

It was high summer and the forests above the fjord were a full, deep green again. The sun glittered across the broad water as though there had never been winter in the world, and would never be winter again. The blue-grey woodsmoke rose straight up from the cottages that lay along the shore, and children ran after each other, brandishing sticks for swords.

Behind the huts, tethered cattle grazed on what they could find. The pigs, as ever, rooted cheekily wherever they wished and only lost their smug air of self-confidence when the headman's dog, Brann, ran out from his master's hut and chased them grunting away.

Outside the headman's hut sat three men, on a bench in the morning sun. Old Thorn cupped his horny hand about his ear to hear what was being said. He paid great attention, like an aged but earnest scholar. Sigurd sat attentive too. One of his legs was still bound thickly with a flannel wrapping and he carried a stout blackthorn staff. These men listened to the one who sat between them. He was a raw-boned young man, his light hair cropped short, his lithe body dressed in a simple rough tunic of linen. He was talking gravely and with a quiet confidence. The old men nodded as he spoke. Sometimes he would make a wide gesture with his hand, as though explaining something, when the others would follow his every movement with their pale-blue eyes, as though they were hungry for information. Then they would nod and smile at each other, having understood his words.

At length a young girl came out of the hut, bearing a big clay pannikin of milk. She offered it to Thorn first, but he waved her aside. She stood irresolute for a moment, about to offer it to Sigurd. Then her father spoke, almost in reproof, 'Give it to the viking, girl,' he said testily. 'Give it to Harald Sigurdson. He has been where none of us will ever go. He has come back to us from the belly of the sea.'

The young man looked down. 'We lost your longship, headman,' he said.

Thorn looked across the fjord to where the woodsmoke rose from another settlement.

'A ship can be built again,' he said. 'But a true man once lost is lost for ever.'

After a while Sigurd said, 'They are building a longship over there. Will you go and take the knuckle-bones from her master?'

Harald looked down at his deeply scarred hands. He felt the itch of the wounds across his back as he leaned against the wall of the hut. His mind suddenly flung him the picture of his white fingers slipping from the curragh's rim.

'Maybe, maybe, father,' he said. 'Who knows? There is time. But come what may, one day I would wish to talk with John's brothers again, to tell them about him.'

Thorn said, 'You have sailed with men, viking. The world will never see their like again.'

Harald smiled sadly, 'Who can tell, headman?' he said. 'Perhaps there will be others as good. Perhaps one day

their longships will sail the seas as thick as seeds on a lake.'

'Hm, perhaps,' said Thorn, taking the milk-bowl, 'but I doubt it.'

Harald's father said, 'I have a hankering to go where you have been, son. Perhaps to make a home alongside Olaf on Orkney.'

The old headman said, 'I have often told you, Sigurd, that there is always a home for you here, by the fjord. Will that not do for you?'

Just then a fresh breeze blew in from seawards, carrying on it the sharp tang of salt. Two white gulls swooped up from the blue waters and on over the pine woods above the village, and out of sight. Sigurd sniffed the air and followed the flight of the birds.

'Ah, they are free creatures,' he said, still looking up. 'My leg is much better than it was, since seeing you, Harald. Perhaps if we waste no time we shall be there before they launch her.'

He put his hand on his son's strong shoulder and stretched his leg, trying it.

Thorn looked bewildered. 'Where are you going?' he said. 'Are you not happy here?'

Sigurd and Harald smiled back at him gently and then gazed over the fjord to where the longship was a-building.

Old Thorn shook his head sorrowfully, 'Ah, vikings! Vikings!' he mumbled. 'There's no understanding them. They are tied to salt-water as a prisoner is tied with chains! No, there's no understanding them! They're either madmen – or heroes!'

He called his daughter to lead him back into the warmth of the hut. He was still shaking his head.